LIFE-CHANGING STORIES OF

COMING OF Age

LIFE-CHANGING STORIES OF

COMING OF Age

EDITED BY **THOMAS DYJA**

ILLUMINA™

MARLOWE & COMPANY
NEW YORK

LIFE-CHANGING STORIES OF COMING OF AGE

Compilation copyright © 2001 by Avalon Publishing Group Incorporated
Introductions copyright © 2001 by Avalon Publishing Group Incorporated

Illumina™ and the Illumina™ logo are trademarks of
Avalon Publishing Group Incorporated.

Published by
Marlowe & Company
A Division of Avalon Publishing Group Incorporated
161 William Street, 16th floor
New York, NY 10038

A Balliett & Fitzgerald book

An Illumina Book ™

Book design: Jennifer Daddio and Michael Walters

Library of Congress Catalog-in-Publication Data

Life-changing stories of coming of age/edited by Thomas Dyja.
        p. cm.—(Illumina)
    ISBN 1-56924-576-2 (pbk.)
    1. Adolescence—Fiction. 2. Maturation (Psychology)—Fiction. 3. Life
change events—Fiction. 4.Youth—Fiction. 5. American fiction. I. Dyja,
Tom. II. Series.

PS648.A34 L54 2001
808.83'9354 –dc21   2001044424

9 8 7 6 5 4 3 2 1

Manufactured in the United States of America

Distributed by Publishers Group West

CONTENTS

LETTER FROM THE EDITOR

Many believe that literature cannot change the world, that it should be content to live between its covers, on the shelves, as a decoration to our lives.

But at the most difficult, challenging, complex moments, again and again we reach up to those shelves, finding guidance and solace and drive among the words of great writers. While a novel may not topple a government, it can change hearts, stiffen resolve, light fires, dry tears or cause them to flow and so affect the world along with the millions of other small motions, the seed-carrying breezes and rivulets, that make our planet work.

We have created Illumina Books in hopes of changing your life. Maybe not in earth-shattering ways, but in ways that comfort and inspire, in ways that help you to continue on.

Each Illumina anthology is a careful collection of extraordinary writing related to a very specific yet universal moment; bouncing back from a lost love, for example, or the journey to healing. With the greatest authors as your guides, you'll read the stories of those who have traveled the same road, learn what they did, see how they survived and moved on.

By offering you the focused beauty and wisdom of this literature, we think Illumina Books can have a powerful, even a therapeutic effect. They're meant not just to work on the mind, but in the heart and soul as well.

—The Editor

from

THE ROAD FROM COORAIN

JILL KER CONWAY

To come of age is to be figuratively thrust out of the
garden, but in the case of Jill Ker Conway it was also
literally so. While the Australian Outback hardly
seems an Eden, it was, for a time, the scene of her
happy childhood. Then, when a tragic drought
turned the rugged Outback into an enemy, she was
forced off the land and into the bitter realities of life
and death.

After the great rain of 1939, the rainfall declined noticeably in each successive year. In 1940, the slight fall was of no consequence because our major worry was that the accumulation of growth on the land would produce serious bushfires. These did occur on land quite close to us, but my father's foresight in getting cattle to eat down the high grass preserved Coorain from that danger.

In 1941, the only rain of the year was a damp cold rain with high wind which came during the lambing season in May and June and carried off many ewes and their newborn lambs. After that there were no significant rainfalls for five years. The unfolding of a drought of these dimensions has a slow and inexorable quality. The weather perpetually holds out hope. Storm clouds gather. Thunder rolls by. But nothing happens. Each year as the season for rain approaches, people begin to look hopefully up at the sky. It mocks them with a few showers, barely enough to lay the dust. That is all.

It takes a long time for a carefully managed grazing property to decline, but three years without rain will do it. Once the disaster begins it unfolds swiftly. So it was with us.

My parents, buoyed up by the good year of 1939, the results of that good year returned in the 1940 wool sales, the new water supply, and the new woolshed, remained hopeful for a long time. By 1942, it was apparent that the drought could be serious and their levels of anxiety began to climb. I was conscious of those anxieties in a variety of ways. That year, 1942, my eighth, was my first one of correspondence school. There was no governess, nor was there any pretense that I would keep a daily school schedule. On Friday afternoons, from 2:00 p.m. until I finished (usually around 4:30 p.m.), I did my week's school. My mother made it a pleasant occasion for me by saying, "Today, you don't have to work out of doors. You can sit in the shade [or if it was winter, in the sun] on the veranda, have your own pot of tea, and do your schoolwork." Thus I was introduced to study as a leisure activity, a gift beyond price. When I was close to finishing, my mother would arrive to glance quickly over the work. Then she questioned me closely about the state of each paddock, what my father had said about it when we were there last, and then, ever so discreetly, she would lead me to talk about how he had seemed as we worked together that week. I needed no instruction not to mention these conversations. I knew why she was anxious.

My father and I would set out to work on horseback as usual, but instead of our customary cheerful and wide-ranging conversations he would be silent. As we looked at sheep, or tried to assess the pasture left in a particular paddock, he would swear softly, looking over the fence to a neighbor's property, already eaten out and beginning to blow sand. Each time he said, "If it doesn't rain, it will bury this feed in a few weeks." It was true and I could think of nothing consoling to say.

His usual high spirits declined with the state of the land, until the terrible day when many of our own sheep were lost because of a sudden cold rain and wind when they had too little food in their stomachs. Although my mother produced her usual ample meals, he began to lose weight his bony frame could ill afford. He lost his wonderful calm, and deliberation in planning, and would be excited by the slightest sign of trouble. A few years ago, a bore losing water flow would have meant there was a problem with the pump, requiring some days' labor to repair it. Now he would instantly worry about whether the water supply was running dry. We would fall to work on raising the pump and assessing the problem as though disaster were at hand.

My mother was impatient with this excitability and in my father's presence, would try to deflate it. But I knew from her questions that she too was worried. When the work to be done on the run didn't need two people, my father would say, "Stay home and help your mother, she needs help in the house." My mother would let him set out for the stables or the garage and then say to me, "I don't need help. Run quickly and go with your father. See if you can make him laugh." So I would set out, and begin to play the child I no longer was. I would think up nonsense rhymes, ask crazy questions, demand to be told stories, invent some of my own to recount. Sometimes it would have the desired effect, but it was hard to distract a man from the daily deterioration of our land and flocks. Every time we stopped to look at the carcass of a dead sheep and dismounted to find out why it had died, it became more difficult to play my role.

My brothers would return home from boarding school to a household consumed with anxiety. Coming, as they did, from the totally enclosed world of a school, with its boyish high spirits, it was hard for them to change emotional gear and set immediately to work on whatever projects had been saved for a time when there were several extra pairs of strong hands available. Mealtimes were particularly difficult because inevitably their world contained many points of reference beyond Coorain. Much of what they reported seemed frivolous to parents who had never attended a fashionable school and had struggled for the considerable learning they possessed. In better times they might have entered enthusiastically into this new world of their sons, but my father in particular jumped to the conclusion that his sons were not working hard at school. In fact they were, but they now lived in a culture in which it was a serious *faux pas* to indicate that one worked hard at study. The two worlds were not easy to mesh. As a result, the boys tended to work together; or we three made our recreations as unobtrusively as possible away from the adult world. Bob's passion was electronics. We spent hours together winding coils and puzzling our way through the diagrams which guided the construction of his first short-wave radio. He instructed me patiently in the characteristics of radio waves, and explained elementary concepts in physics by duplicating many of the demonstrations in his school textbooks. Barry took me with him on his early morning trips to collect the rabbits and foxes he trapped to help control these populations, which were hazards to our sheep. The skins provided him pocket money for investment in a wide variety of projects. While he was home from school, guides on writing short stories, books on muscle building, magazines about automobiles lent the mail bag an excitement lacking at other times.

There was not much room in the household routine for the mood swings and questioning of adolescence. Discipline was strict, and departures from it earned immediate punishment. The cloud of parental disapproval could be heavy when there was no escaping to other society. At sixteen, Bob let slip his religious doubts during a lunchtime conversation. Though these were a logical consequence of his heavily scientific school program, my parents were outraged. They had expected that by sending him to a high Anglican school, his religious education was ensured. Religious belief was a touchy subject in the family because my father adhered to his Catholicism while my mother was outspoken in her criticism of Catholic ideas on sexuality and the subordination of women. There was little occasion for the expression of these differences because there was no place of worship in either faith within seventy to a hundred miles of Coorain. Still, the differences slumbered under the surface. Poor Bob was treated as an unnatural being for his doubts and accused of being ungrateful for the sacrifices made to send him to a religious school. I was glad when the boys returned safely to school a week later without more explosions of discord. I was puzzled about the whole question of religion myself, since my parents both seemed highly moral people to me. As both faiths seemed to produce excellent results, I did not know what to make of the difference. When we made one of our rare visits to Sydney, and my parents separated for the day, my mother to shop, my father to visit banks and wool merchants, I usually went with him, since I got tired and vexed my mother by complaining while she rushed to do a year's shopping in a matter of days. At the end of the day, before setting out for our hotel or flat, my father would stop at St. Mary's Cathedral for vespers. I liked the ritual and the Latin chant. I also understood when he said it would be better not to mention these visits to my mother.

The routine of the academic year required that the boys return to school at the end of the summer vacation before the periods of most intense activity on the property: crutching time in February (when only the withers of the sheep were shorn to limit fly infestation in hot weather) and shearing in early June. Crutching time in 1943 was particularly worrisome. It was a fearfully hot summer. The sheep were poorly nourished and the last season's lambs weak. They needed to be moved slowly, held in paddocks close to the sheepyards, crutched quickly, and returned to their sparse pastures before heat exhaustion took its toll. In addition, to speed the whole process, someone needed to be at the woolshed, counting each shearer's tally of sheep, and pushing the supply of animals into the shed, so that not a moment was lost. It was always an exhausting business, because speed required constant running about in the 100 degree weather. This year, it was clear that my father found it hard to bear the pace.

At home in the evening, I found my mother feeling his pulse, administering brandy, and urging him to lie down. The heat and anxiety had combined to revive the irregular heartbeat that had been one of the factors occasioning his discharge from the army in 1917. My mother was at her best caring for the sick. She radiated calm. The errant pulse was checked regularly and diagnosed as palpitations, but not a serious arrhythmia.

The next day, we went a little more slowly at the work in the yards, advised by my mother that we could still afford to keep the team an extra day or two, or lose a few sheep, provided that my father was in sound health. I now found myself volunteering for jobs I was not quite sure I could do, in order to be sure that he had more time to rest. The next afternoon, after the close of work at the shed, there was a lot of riding still to be done. "These sheep need to go to Rigby's, that mob to Denny's," my father began, about to give me an assignment to return sheep to their paddocks. "I can do both," I said rashly, having never moved so many sheep on my own. "Mind you, move them slowly, and don't let them mix with the rams. Take the dogs, and don't open the gate until you have the dogs holding them at the fence." He had forgotten that I couldn't remount easily, and that the dogs didn't work very well for me. I was half pleased at completing the two assignments, half astonished that anyone had left me to handle them alone. Too much is being asked of me, I thought privately, forgetting that it was I who had volunteered. There was no getting around that the work was there and had to be done, and so I fell early into a role it took me many years to escape, the person in the family who would rise to the occasion, no matter the size of the task.

Shortly afterwards, the first terrible dust storm arrived boiling out of the central Australian desert. One sweltering late afternoon in March, I walked out to collect wood for the stove. Glancing toward the west, I saw a terrifying sight. A vast boiling cloud was mounting in the sky, black and sulfurous yellow at the heart, varying shades of ocher red at the edges. Where I stood, the air was utterly still, but the writhing cloud was approaching silently and with great speed. Suddenly I noticed that there were no birds to be seen or heard. All had taken shelter. I called my mother. We watched helplessly. Always one for action, she turned swiftly, went indoors, and began to close windows. Outside, I collected the buckets, rakes, shovels, and other implements that could blow away or smash a window if hurled against one by the boiling wind. Within the hour, my father arrived home. He and my mother sat on the back step, not in their usual restful contemplation, but silenced instead by dread.

A dust storm usually lasts days, blotting out the sun, launching banshee winds day and night. It is dangerous to stray far from shelter, because the sand and grit lodge in one's eyes, and a visibility often reduced to a few feet can make one completely disoriented. Animals which become exhausted and lie down are often sanded over and smothered. There is nothing anyone can do but stay inside, waiting for the calm after the storm. Inside, it is stifling. Every window must be closed against the dust, which seeps relentlessly through the slightest crack. Meals are gritty and sleep elusive. Rising in the morning, one sees a perfect outline of one's body, an afterimage of white where the dust has not collected on the sheets.

As the winds seared our land, they took away the dry herbage, piled it against the fences, and then slowly began to silt over the debris. It was three days before we could venture out, days of almost unendurable tension. The crashing of the boughs of trees against our roof and the sharp roar as a nearly empty rainwater tank blew off its stand and rolled away triggered my father's recurring nightmares of France, so that when he could fall into a fitful slumber it would be to awake screaming.

It was usually I who woke him from his nightmares. My mother was hard to awaken. She had, in her stoic way, endured over the years two bad cases of ear infection, treated only with our available remedies, hot packs and aspirin. One ear was totally deaf as a result of a ruptured eardrum, and her hearing in the other ear was much reduced. Now her deafness led to a striking reversal of roles, as I, the child in the family, would waken and attempt to soothe a frantic adult.

When we emerged, there were several feet of sand piled up against the windbreak to my mother's garden, the contours of new sandhills were beginning to form in places where the dust eddied and collected. There was no question that there were also many more bare patches where the remains of dry grass and herbage had lifted and blown away.

It was always a miracle to me that animals could endure so much. As we checked the property, there were dead sheep in every paddock to be sure, but fewer than I'd feared. My spirits began to rise and I kept telling my father the damage was not too bad. "That was only the first storm," he said bleakly. He had seen it all before and knew what was to come.

In June, at shearing time, we hired one of the district's

great eccentrics to help in the yards. I could not manage mustering and yard work at the same time, and my father could not manage both either without too frenetic a pace. Our helper, known as Pommy Goodman, was a middle-aged Englishman with a perfect Mayfair accent, one of the foulest mouths I ever heard, and the bearing of one to the manner born. He was an example of the wonderful variety of types thrown up like human driftwood on the farther shores of settlement in Australia. One moment he would be swearing menacingly at a sheep that had kicked him, the next minute addressing me as though he were my nanny and about to order nursery tea. I resented being called "child," and noticed that Pommy did more leaning on the fence and offering advice than hard work. But it was good to have a third person on hand, and especially someone who could drive a car, something I could not do, my legs not yet being long enough to disengage a clutch. Pommy could drive ahead and open a gate, making the return of sheep to a paddock a simple task. He could shuttle between the house and woolshed on the endless errands that materialized during the day, and he could count out the sheep from the shearers' pens, something I was not good at because my mathematical labors by correspondence were always done slowly and deliberately. The sheep raced for freedom at a furious pace, leaping through the gate in twos and threes, so that my counts were often jumbled. The shearers, by now old friends, knowing that my father was not well, tolerated my efforts and secretly kept their own tally, so the records were straight at the end of the day.

After helping at crutching time, Pommy, by now a friend to me, took the job of postmaster at our little post office and manual telephone exchange in Mossgiel. There he was as bossy as he had been to me in the sheepyards, listening to everyone's conversations, offering his own comments at crucial points in people's communication, and opening and closing the service at arbitrary hours. It soon became clear that he was drinking heavily, alone every night in the postmaster's cramped quarters. His slight frame grew emaciated and when I came with my father to the post office he barely had the spirit to correct my grammar. One morning, about three months after he left us, the exchange was dead. No one paid much attention, thinking that he was taking longer than usual to sober up. His first customer of the day found him swinging from the central beam of the post office, fully dressed in suit and tie. He had been sober enough to arrange the noose efficiently and kick the chair he stood on well across the room. I could never go there again without eyeing the beam and wondering about his thoughts that night. What old sorrows had overwhelmed him? Or was he simply a victim of loneliness and depression? I wondered whether his inner dialogue that night was in the voice of a cultivated Englishman, or in that of a foul-mouthed drover. He came to be one of my symbols for our need for society, and of the folly of believing that we can manage our fate alone.

I was used to worry about my father's health and state of mind, but it was a shock in the spring of 1943 to learn that my mother must go to Sydney for a hysterectomy, surgery that, in the current state of Australian medicine, still required months of recuperation. She left for Sydney shortly before the boys arrived home from school for the Christmas holidays. I was sent for an anticipated month's stay with friends who lived thirty miles away from us on a station with the poetic name Tooralee. My hosts had an only child, a daughter, then about five years old, and slow to speak for lack of the talkative child company my visit was to supply. My mother was, in fact, away for eight weeks. She had caught a cold the day before entering the hospital for her surgery, and that infection had progressed quickly to pneumonia, a dangerous infection in the period before antibiotics or sulfa drugs. When she returned, stepping off the silver-painted diesel train in Ivanhoe into a temperature of 108 degrees, she was startlingly pale and thin. My father began to order us to lift packages, to jump to do the household chores, and to work in our amateurish way at tending her garden. She refused all well-intentioned efforts to make her an invalid. "My surgeon says his stitches are very strong," she said. "I can lift anything. I will have all my energy back in three months." So she did; but we never again saw the rosy-cheeked, robust woman of our childhood. She remained painfully thin.

As we entered the late summer of 1944, we had about half our usual stock of sheep, now seriously affected by inadequate nourishment. It was clear that they would not make it through the summer unless it rained, or we began to feed them hay or grain to supplement their diet. The question which tormented my parents was whether to let them die, or invest more in maintaining them. If they died, fifteen years of careful attention to the bloodlines was lost. Yet even if fed supplements they might die anyway, for the dry feed would not supply the basic nutrients in fresh grass and herbage.

Now the nighttime conversations were anguished. Both of them had grown up fearing debt like the plague. It hurt their pride to mortgage the land, just like more feckless managers. Furthermore, the feeding would require more labor than my father and I could manage. In the end, it was resolved to borrow the money, buy the wheat, and hire the help. But these actions were taken with a heavy heart. My father was plagued by doubts about the wisdom of the decision. My mother, once settled on a course of action, was imperturbable. Their basic difference of temperament was that she lacked imagination and could not conceive of failure, while my father's imagination now tormented him with ever darker visions of disaster. She regarded this fevered imagination dourly and thought it should be controllable. He tried to keep his worst fears to himself.

Our help came in the wonderful form of two brothers, half aboriginal, half Chinese. The elder brother, Ron, in his early twenties, was light-skinned and slightly slant-eyed; the younger, Jack, looked like a full-blooded aboriginal. They came from the mission station in Menindee, one hundred and seventy miles away. They were as fine a pair of station hands as one could ever hope for. Ron could fix engines and manage all things mechanical. He was quiet, efficient, and totally dependable. Jack could talk to animals, soothe a frightened horse, persuade half-starving sheep to get up and keep walking. Jack could pick up a stone and toss it casually to knock down out of the sky the crows gathering around a foundered animal. He could track anything: snakes, sheep, kangaroos, lizards. Jack's only defect so far as station management was concerned was that at any time he might feel the aboriginal need to go "on walkabout." He was utterly reliable and would always reappear to complete the abandoned task he'd been at work on when the urge came. But he could be gone for days, or weeks, or months.

Feeding the sheep was hard work. Feed troughs made of metal could not be considered because the drifting sand would quickly cover them. If the weaker sheep were to get their nourishment, the expanse of feeding troughs must be large so that every animal would have its chance at the grain.

So we settled on burlap troughs hung on wire—light enough for the wind to blow beneath when empty, cheap enough to produce in hundred-foot lengths. Replacement lengths became available each time we emptied a hundredweight bag of wheat. With a bag needle and a hank of twine at hand anyone could mend the troughs, or with a little wire and some wooden pegs, create new ones.

When we began our feeding program in the troughs placed by major watering places, the sheep seemed only slowly to discover the grain. Within a few weeks the hungry animals would stampede at the sight of anyone carrying bags of wheat, and someone had to be sent as a decoy to draw them off in search of a small supply of grain while the major ration was being poured into the troughs. Since I could carry only twenty pounds at a fast run, I was the decoy while the men carried forty- and fifty-pound bags on their shoulders to empty into the feeding troughs. At first the sheep were ravenous but measured in following the decoy. Soon they would race so hard toward the grain that they would send the decoy flying unless he or she outraced them. Then they would pause, wheel on catching the scent of the ration in the troughs, and stampede back toward the food.

Our principal enemies as we carried out this daily process were the pink cockatoos and crows, which tore the burlap to pieces in search of the grains of wheat left behind. Soon the mending of the troughs was a daily task, a task made miserable by the blowflies, the blistering sun, the blowing sand, and the stench of the bodies of the sheep for whom the wheat had arrived too late.

For my father each death was a personal blow, and he took himself to task for the suffering of the animals. Our conversations as we rode about the place took on a grimmer tone. "When I'm gone, Jill, sell this place. Take care of your mother. Make sure she goes to the city. There's nothing but heartbreak in fighting the seasons." Or, "If anything happens to me, promise me you'll take care of your mother. Make her sell this place. Don't let her stay here." I would promise anything to change his mood and get the conversation on another topic. But I rarely succeeded. Usually he would go on to talk about my future, a future in which he clearly did not expect to share. "Work hard, Jill," he'd say. "Don't just waste time. *Make something of yourself.*" Reverting to his idée fixe that my brothers did not try hard enough at their school-work, he would continue, "Don't be like your brothers. Don't waste your time in school. Get a real education and get away from this damn country for good." I would promise, choking back tears at the thought of his death and a future away from Coorain. But even I could see that he was right about the battle with the seasons. Without discussing the subject with anyone, I concluded that the God who was supposed to heed the fall of the sparrow had a lesser morality than humans. Each clap of dry thunder and each vista of starving animals made the notion of a loving God a mockery. I kept my father's words about impending death to myself. I was used to being the listener to fears and worries my parents needed to express, but did not want to worry one another about. It seemed too monstrous a possibility to speak about, and in a primitive way I feared that naming it might make it happen.

One troublesome aspect of the frustration of my parents' dreams was the extent to which they transferred their ambitions to their children. My brothers, being five hundred miles away, were not readily available as vehicles for ambition. Being at hand, I became the focus of all the aspiration for achievement that had fueled both parents' prodigious energies. My correspondence school required little of my time and less energy. My teacher's reports were always positive and my work praised. Naturally, it should have been, for I had heard the same lessons discussed in the schoolroom by my brothers and their governess.

I read omnivorously, everything that came to hand, and through reading my mother's books I asked questions about politics and history which both parents took for signs of high intelligence. Lacking playmates, I would retreat from the adult world to my swing, set away in the eucalyptus trees a hundred yards or so from the house. There I would converse at length with imaginary companions, usually characters from some recently read novel or war correspondent's report, which I only dimly understood. I would kick furiously in order to rise up higher and see a little farther beyond the horizon. In the midst of my dreams of glory drawn from highly glamorized accounts of war and feats of heroism, I would sometimes stop crestfallen and wonder if I would ever get away from Coorain. Sometimes, needing to be alone, I would walk for hours, scanning the ground for aboriginal ovens, collecting quartz fragments, observing the insect life—anything to be away from the house and its overwhelming mood of worry.

The nighttime conversations now made me nervous because they frequently settled on what a remarkable child I was, and how gratifying it would be for parents to observe my progress. I had no way of assessing their judgments, but I was certainly uncomfortably aware that I and my performance in life had become the focus of formidable emotional energies.

Like all children, I was occasionally mischievous and misbehaved. In more carefree times my pranks, like my brothers', met with swift punishment from parents who believed that sparing the rod was certain to spoil the child. The occasional token chastisement was easy to resist psychologically. One had only to refuse to apologize and express contrition for enough hours to gain the upper hand on parents who were tired in the evening and wanted to go to bed. Now, however, I encountered more subtle, and to me more terrifying, punishments. If I misbehaved, my parents simply acted as though I were not their child but a stranger. They would inquire civilly as to who I was and what I was doing on Coorain, but no hint of recognition escaped them. This treatment never failed to reduce me to abject contrition. In later life my recurring nightmares were always about my inability to prove to people I knew quite well who I was. I became an unnaturally good child, and accepted uncritically that goodness was required of me if my parents' disappointments in life were ever to be compensated for.

That June most of our older sheep were too weak to be shorn. My father took the few whose wool was worth shearing and who could stand the journey to a neighboring station, since the numbers were too small to warrant bringing a shearing team to Coorain. On the first day of his absence, my mother also left in the afternoon to pick up the mail and carry out some other errands. I had time to fulfill an often neglected promise to my brother Bob that I would listen on his shortwave radio every afternoon and record the stations and countries I heard. That day, the sixth of June, I turned the dial to the point where we had discovered that we could hear the uncensored news being dictated to General MacArthur's headquarters. To my astonishment, I heard the impassive announcer's voice report the news of the Allied landing in Normandy, and the establishment of beachheads beyond Utah and Omaha beaches literally only a few hours earlier. By the time my mother returned in the late afternoon, I was gibbering with excitement and almost incoherent with my news. She listened carefully, sorted out the story, and promised to tell my father when he telephoned that evening. This she did, although the evening Australian news contained no report of the landing. I was not vindicated until the six o'clock news the following night, when the Australian censors decided to release the news of the successful landings. Thereafter, no matter what the circumstances on Coorain, I could always distract my father by reading him reports of the campaign on the various fronts in Europe as we jolted about Coorain in our sulky, traveling to clean watering troughs or mend our feeding troughs. I could supplement the newspaper accounts by the more accurate reporting which I heard on my brother's radio, where the actual figures of casualties were reported rather than the bland announcements made for civilian consumption. Reading about the invasion in Europe was reassuring because our own situation in Australia had grown more precarious as the war in the Pacific unfolded.

We had been jolted out of complacency by the fall of Singapore, the supposedly impregnable British naval base, fortified with guns which pointed only out to sea. My mother and I had been on a brief trip to Sydney when Singapore fell. The newspaper headlines covered the whole front page of the afternoon dailies. So great was the shock that Australians, the most taciturn of people, had actually been moved to speak about the news to total strangers. Handfuls of refugees began to arrive from Hong Kong, but there were none from Singapore, except the Australian commander, Major-General Gordon Bennett, who we were ashamed to learn had deserted his men. Many of our friends and sons of friends had been in the Australian contingent at Singapore, including our fondly remembered Jimmie Walker. We had his smiling picture in his A.I.F. uniform sent just before his departure. The news of Japanese treatment of prisoners and the atrocities committed upon the civilian population of the Philippines made the increasing likelihood of the invasion of Australia seem more threatening.

My parents' conversations on this possibility were chilling but practical. Australia was drained of able-bodied men, away fighting in Europe and the Middle East. These two proudly loyal subjects of the British crown had thrilled to the sound of Churchill's speeches hurling defiance at Hitler, invoking the glory of the British Empire to inspire the defense of England. They were correspondingly shaken to realize that Australia was expendable in Britain's war strategy, and that the Australian government had had great difficulty in securing the return of the battle-scarred Ninth Division from Tobruk to take part in the defense of Australia. Once this was clear they turned soberly to consideration of what to do in the event of an invasion. They calculated correctly that the continent was too vast to be easily overrun, that the Japanese would concentrate on the ports and the food supplies. We, who were hardy backcountry people, could disappear if need be into the great outback desert and live off the land like aborigines. There were various plans for getting the boys home, and discussions about how that might be achieved in a time of likely national panic. When the call came for civilians to turn over all their hunting rifles to the government to help arm the militia, a pitifully small group of men who had refused to serve overseas when drafted, my father kept back one of his rifles and hid it with a supply of ammunition. If we were ever in danger of capture, he and my mother had calmly agreed that he would shoot his wife and children first and then himself. In preparation for such dire possibilities, we hid supplies in a remote part of Coorain. The gasoline was described as a cache to be reserved for emergencies, and we never spoke about the need for a weapon.

We had very realistic expectations about the defense of Australia, because it was patently apparent that there was a failure of leadership in the country, symbolized by Major-General Gordon Bennett's ignominious flight, the flustered performance of the first wartime leader, the United Australian Party Prime Minister Robert Menzies, and the short-lived Country Party government which followed. The task of defending the country was impossible for Australians alone, and the old empire mentalities of our leaders left them, without the protection of Great Britain, as paralyzed as the defenders of Singapore. My parents were rugged individualists who scorned socialism and the Labor Party as the political recourse of those who lacked initiative. Nonetheless, their spirits soared when the Labor Prime Minister, John Curtin, took office, candidly acknowledged our situation, and called for American assistance. They recognized an Australian patriot, and I learned for the first time that loyalty to Great Britain and love for Australia were not synonymous. It was an important lesson.

After the June shearing of 1944, we knew that if it did not rain in the spring our gamble was lost. The sheep would not live through until another rainy season. There were so few to feed by September 1944 that our friends and helpers, Ron and Jack Kelly, left for another job. We on Coorain waited for the rain which never came. The dust storms swept over us every two or three weeks, and there was no pretending about the state of the sheep when we traveled around the property. The smells of death and the carrion birds were everywhere. The starving animals which came to our feed troughs were now demented with hunger. When I ran off as decoy to spread out a thin trail of grain while the troughs were filled, they knocked me over and trampled me, desperate to tear the grain from the bag. Their skeletal bodies were pitiful. I found I could no longer bear to look into their eyes, because the usually tranquil ruminant animals looked half crazed.

We lost our appetite for meat because the flesh of the starving animals already tasted putrid. I was never conscious of when the smell of rotting animals drowned out the perfumes from my mother's garden, but by early December, although it still bloomed, our nostrils registered only decaying flesh. By then the sand accumulating on the other side of the windbreak was beginning to bend the cane walls inward by its weight, and we knew it was only a matter of time before it too was engulfed.

My mother, as always, was unconquerable. "It has to rain some day," she told my father. "Our children are healthy. We can grow our food. What does it matter if we lose everything else?" She did not understand that it mattered deeply to him. Other memories of loss from his childhood were overwhelming him. He could not set out in mid-life to be once more the orphan without patrimony. As he sank into deeper depression, they understood one another less. She, always able to rouse herself to action, could not understand how to deal with crippling depression, except by a brisk call to count one's blessings. This was just what my father was unable to do.

My brothers were summoned home two weeks early from school, though to help with what was not clear. There was pitifully little to do on Coorain. There were the same burlap troughs to mend, the same desperate animals to feed, but the size of the task was shrinking daily. The December heat set in, each day over 100 degrees. Now so much of our land was without vegetation that the slightest breeze set the soil blowing. Even without the dust storms, our daily life seemed lived in an inferno.

My mother's efforts to rouse my father were indefatigable. One Saturday in early December was to be a meeting of the Pastures Protection Board in Hillston. Early in the week before, she set about persuading him to drive the seventy-five miles with his close friend Angus Waugh. Reluctantly, he agreed. The Friday before, a minor dust storm set in, and he decided against the drive. It was fearfully hot, over 108 degrees, and we passed a fitful evening barricaded in against the blowing sand.

The next morning I awoke, conscious that it was very early, to find my father gazing intently at me. He bent down to embrace me and said good-bye. Half asleep, I bid him good-bye and saw his departing back. Suddenly, I snapped awake. *Why is he saying good-bye? He isn't going anywhere.* I leapt out of bed, flung on the first clothes to hand, and ran dry-mouthed after him. I was only seconds too late. I ran shouting after his car, "I want to come. Take me with you." I thought he saw me, but, the car gathering speed, he drove away.

Back in the house, my mother found me pacing about and asked why I was up so early in the morning. I said I'd wanted to go with my father, and wasn't sure where he went. He was worried about the heat and the adequacy of the water for the sheep in Brooklins (a distant paddock), she said, and had gone to check on it. It was a hot oppressive day, with the wind gaining strength by noon. I felt a leaden fear in my stomach, but was speechless. To speak of my fears seemed to admit that my father had lost his mental balance. It was something I could not say.

His journey should not have taken more than two hours, but then again he could have decided to visit other watering places on the property. When he was not home by two, my mother and Bob set out after him. Neither Barry nor I, left behind, was inclined to talk about what might have happened. Like a pair of automatons, we washed the dishes left from lunch and settled in to wait. When no one returned by four, the hour when my mother stoked the stove and began her preparations for dinner, we went through the motions of her routine. The potatoes were peeled, peas shelled, the roast prepared, the table laid.

Eventually, Bob arrived home alone. There had been an accident, he said. He must make some phone calls and hurry back. We neither of us believed him. We knew my father was dead. Finally, at six o'clock, the old grey utility my father drove hove into sight driven by my brother Bob; my mother's car followed, with several others in its wake. She took the time to thank us for preparing dinner before saying she had something to tell us alone. We went numbly to our parents' bedroom, the place of all confidential conversations. "I want you to help me," she said. "Your father's dead. He was working on extending the piping into the Brooklins dam. We found him there in the water." My eyes began to fill with tears. She looked at me accusingly. "Your father wouldn't want you to cry," she said.

We watched woodenly as my father's body was brought to rest in that same bedroom. We were dismissed while she prepared it for the funeral which would take place in two days. In the hot summer months, burials had to be speedy and there was no need for anyone to explain why to us children. We had been dealing with decaying bodies for years. Because of the wartime restrictions on travel and the need for haste, there was little time to summon family and friends. Telegrams were dispatched but only my mother's brother and sister-in-law, close to us in Sydney, were actually expected. Eventually, we sat down to dinner and choked over our food, trying desperately to make conversation with the kindly manager from a neighboring station who had come to help. The meal seemed surreal. The food on the plate seemed unconnected to the unreal world without my father in it in which I now lived. I was haunted by the consciousness of his body lying close by in the bedroom, which my mother had sternly forbidden me to enter.

After we went sleeplessly to bed, we heard a sound never heard before, the sound of my mother weeping hopelessly and inconsolably. It was a terrible and unforgettable sound.

To moderate the heat we slept on a screened veranda exposed to any southern breeze which might stir. My brother Barry's bed was next to mine. After listening to this terrible new sound, we both agreed that we wished we were older so that we could go to work and take care of her. We tossed until the sun rose and crept out of bed too shocked to do more than converse in whispers.

My mother soon appeared, tight-lipped and pale, somehow a ghost of herself. Dispensing with all possibility of discussion, she announced that Barry and I were to stay with friends for a few days. She did not want us to see our father buried, believing that this would be too distressing for us. Though we complied without questioning the plan, I felt betrayed that I would not see him to his last rest. She, for her part, wanted to preserve us from signs of the body's decay. As we set out, driven by the kindly Morison family, who had cared for me during my mother's illness, we passed the hearse making its way toward Coorain. Its black shape drove home what had happened.

How my father's death had actually come about we would never know. He was a poor swimmer, and had attempted to dive down in muddy water to connect a fresh length of pipe so that the pump for watering the sheep could draw from the lowered water level of the dam. It was a diffi-cult exercise for a strong swimmer, and not one to undertake alone. Why he had chosen to do it alone when my two brothers, both excellent swimmers, were at home, we could not understand. I did not tell anyone of his early morning visit to me. I realized that we would never know the answer to the question it raised.

Everyone expected that my mother would sell Coorain, move to the city, and allow a bank or trust company to manage our finances. In our part of the world this was what widows did. Our circle of friends and advisers did not bargain for my mother's business sense and her strong will. She would not sell the property when it was worth next to nothing. She planned instead to run it herself, wait for the rains which must come, and manage our one asset for our maximum benefit. The boys were to return to school according to the usual schedule. She would hire some help, and she and I would remain at Coorain. Presented with this plan and a request to finance it, her startled woolbrokers remonstrated with her about the hazards of a woman taking charge of her own affairs. Seeing her resolve, they acquiesced, and offered her a loan secured by our now virtually nonexistent sheep. So she returned resolute to preserve and enhance the enterprise she and my father had built.

He had not been a man to give much thought to transferring property to wife or children, and so my mother, as his sole heir, became liable for sizable death duties. Some of my first lessons in feminism came from her outraged conversations with the hapless valuation agent sent to inventory and value the assets of the estate for probate. She was incensed to discover that her original investment in furniture, linen, silver, and household equipment was now merged in my father's estate. No value was attributed either to the contributions she had made to the enterprise through the investment of her capital fifteen years before, or to the proceeds of her fifteen years of twelve- and fourteen-hour days of labor. Her outspoken anger cowed the man into some concessions, but her rumblings about this economic injustice continued for years, and instructed me greatly.

Heroic as she was, we would not have fared so well in her defiance of the fates had we not been given the affection, support, and physical presence of my mother's younger brother and his wife. Both worked in essential wartime occupations in Sydney, my uncle as an engineer and my aunt as the senior nurse in a munitions factory. Informed of my father's death, both requested leave to attend his funeral and to help his widow cope with her loss, and both were refused any more than forty-eight hours' absence. In characteristic Australian fashion, they defied the manpower authorities, talked their way onto the train for the west despite the restrictions on civilian travel, and arrived to stay shortly before my father's funeral.

Once they took in the situation my mother faced, they decided to defy the orders they promptly received to return to their respective jobs. Instead, they elected to see her through the harsh first months of bereavement. Their warm hearts, wonderful common sense, and comforting physical presence reassured us children, as my mother grew suddenly thinner, her abundant hair grey almost overnight, and her moods, normally equable, swung to every point of the compass. We struggled through Christmas, trying to celebrate, but at every point in the day we met memories of my father's presence the previous year. At the end of January, the boys left for school, and in late February, my uncle finally obeyed the accumulating pile of telegrams and official letters requiring him to return at once to his wartime post. My aunt remained another month, a calming presence, full of life force, cheerfully sustaining our spirits by her questions about our way of life in a remote part of the country she had never visited. Before my uncle left, our former helper Ron Kelly returned, leaving a much better job to take care of Coorain and us once again.

By the time he arrived, we were feeding only seven or eight hundred sheep in two paddocks, and working to preserve the various improvements, bores, wells, sheepyards, and fences from the encroaching sand. Each day, the three of us went out with our loads of wheat, and to work on the now hated burlap troughs. They were hateful because they had become tattered with much use, and required daily attention with patches, twine, and bag needle. There was no way to make the repairs except to sit down in the dust, thread one's needle, and go at it. With the sun beating down, no hands free to drive away the flies, and the sounds of the ever-hungry and opportunistic cockatoos waiting to tear apart our handiwork, we could not escape awareness of the repetitious and futile nature of our labors.

Each afternoon, Ron set out for another tour of fences: to dig out those sanding up, to treat posts being attacked by white ants under the sand, and to oil and care for all the working parts of the windmills and pumping equipment. At night after the lamps were lit, the silence in the house was palpable. My mother and I read after dinner, but as the time approached for going to bed she would become unaccustomedly nervous and edgy. She found sleeping alone a nightmare, and after a few weeks of sleepless nights she said she needed my company in her bed. After that it was I who had trouble resting, for she clung to me like a drowning person. Alone, without my father, all her fears of the wilderness returned, and she found the silence as alienating as when she first arrived on the plains. She would often pace the verandas much of the night. Both of us would be grateful for the dawn.

Once a week our friend and neighbor Angus Waugh drove the fifty miles to visit us. He would talk over the state of the sheep and the land with my mother, offer sound advice, and try to make her laugh. I longed for his visits so that for even a few hours the care of this silent and grieving person would not rest only on my shoulders. He could always make me laugh by telling wild nonsense stories, or wickedly funny accounts of the life and affairs of distant residents in the district. My mother, in fact, knew in great detail every aspect of the management of a sheep station. Angus knew this very well, but his weekly presence gave her some adult company, and enabled him to keep a watchful and sensitive eye on how we both were faring.

In February, although my mother was uncertain whether she could afford it, the shearing contractor and his team arrived to crutch our sheep. They followed the bush code of helping those in trouble, and told my mother to pay them when she could, or never if it wasn't possible. Help appeared from all quarters at crutching time, and our few poor sheep were back in their paddocks before we knew it. My friends on the team never spoke of our bereavement, but they were even more than usually kind about my efforts to keep on top of everything that was happening at the shed.

By the time the boys came home for their holidays in May it was clear that very few of the animals would survive even if it rained within a few weeks. My brothers shot the few remaining large animals we could not feed—the Black Angus bull, formerly the rippling black embodiment of sexual power and energy, now a wraith; the few poor cows; some starving horses. And then in the next weeks the last sheep began to die by the hundreds. We would pile up the carcasses of those that died near the house, douse them with kerosene, and set them alight, to reduce the pervasive odor of rotting flesh. The crows and hawks were fat, and the cockatoos full-breasted on their diet of wheat, but one by one all other forms of life began to fade away.

After the boys went back to school in June, there was little to do on the place. No amount of digging could prevent the silting-up of fences, and the maintenance of equipment did not require much oversight. Once we were alone again, I was more than usually worried about my mother, because she ate next to nothing, fell to weeping unexpectedly, and seemed much of the time in a trance. The effort expended in getting up and carrying on each day exhausted her. This was combined with the effort expended in refusing to accept the possibility that our enterprise at Coorain might go under. Because this fear was repressed, she was fearful of lesser things. Once when I went riding without telling her, her fury startled me. Once when I went to work on a bore with Ron, an individual who would have died to secure our safety, she gave me a tongue-lashing about never again working alone with him.

Shortly after these explosions, Angus arrived for one of his visits. He took a walk with me and asked how we were doing. As I shook my head, uncertain about how to say what was on my mind, he supplied the words for me. "You're worried about your mother, aren't you," he said. I nodded. "She doesn't eat?"

"That's right," I said. "She's depressed?" I nodded. "You ought to leave here," he said. "There's not a bloody thing you two can do here now. The pair of you look like something out of Changi and it's to no purpose. Would you like to leave, live like a normal child and go to school?" I felt a great wave of relief. "Yes," I said.

That night Angus talked to my mother as they took a walk around the house and grounds. I heard snatches, and realized that he was playing the other side of the argument skillfully. "You can't keep Jill here forever. It's not right. She should be in school. Neither of you can do anything here. Look at her. She's so skinny she could come from a concentration camp. It's time to leave and go to Sydney, and let her get on with her life. You can hire a manager to take care of this place, and I'll watch over it for you."

The next morning my mother eyed me as though I were a stranger. I was certainly a sight. I was in my eleventh year, so underweight my clothes for an eight- or nine-year-old hung on me, and as Angus said, I looked worried enough to be an old woman. Once she noticed my appearance the matter was settled for my mother. She began to make plans for us to leave.

With Angus's help we found a splendid manager. Geoff Coghlan was a thoroughly knowledgeable man about sheep and cattle, and the ways of our western plains country. He had been too young to participate in the 1914–1918 War, and a few years too old to join the armed forces in the

1939–1945 War, then wending toward Allied victory in Europe, and more slowly toward the defeat of Japan in the Pacific. Margaret, his wife, was the daughter of near neighbors, and Coorain offered them a home of their own. Given that my mother would live in Sydney, where I could attend a good school, our new managers would have relative independence to run things their way. It was agreed that they would move to Coorain early in August 1945, and we would depart close to the end of the month.

The actual prospect of departure evoked complicated emotions. The house, the garden, the vistas of space were the only landscape I knew. The ways of the backcountry were second nature, and I associated Sydney with stiff formal clothes, sore feet, and psychological exhaustion from coping with unaccustomed crowds. Yet I knew I could not deal unaided with my mother's grief and despair. As time passed, the energy she had summoned to manage the immediate details of life after my father's death was dissipated, and she sank into a private world of sorrow from which I could not detach her. I was lonely and grief-stricken myself. I had come to hate the sight of the desolate countryside, the whitening bones, and the all-pervasive dust. I, too, was consumed with anxiety because the experience of cumulative disaster had darkened my mood, and made me see the fates as capricious and punishing.

Yet to leave Coorain was almost beyond my comprehension. Each day I prepared myself for the departure by trying to engrave on my memory images that would not fade—the dogs I loved best, the horse I rode, the household cat, the shapes of trees. Ever since my father's death I had called his figure and voice to mind each morning as I woke, determined not to let it fade. Now I did the same with each familiar detail of life. It was strange to hear my mother and Mrs. Coghlan discuss what equipment should stay at Coorain, what china and glass should go with us. The familiar shapes of pots and pans, the patterns on the china— all took on a life of their own. Hitherto they had been simple aspects of the world that was.

Before we left, we made a visit to Clare Station, some fifty miles to the west, to spend two nights with Angus, his sister Eileen, and his younger brother Ron. Their parents had taken up a vast acreage in the 1880s, moving out onto the plains driving their sheep before them, transporting their belongings in bullock wagons. Clare, as they had named their property, had once been larger than its current five hundred thousand acres. It had been so large it was virtually a small town, with such extensive stables and accommodations that it could comfortably serve as a stop for the Cobb and Company coaches which traveled the west before the railroad and the automobile. The second generation of the Waughs were a formidable Scottish clan, thrifty, hardworking, generous, excellent businessmen. I had never seen anything at once so

large and at the same time so haphazard. The station home-
stead was organized around a courtyard, three sides of which
were bedrooms and bathrooms, arranged in no order I could
discern. One walked across a second courtyard to the vast
dining room, itself a good five-minute walk from the kitchens,
set well away in case of fire. Everyone laughed about the fact
that this inconvenient distance made the meals always luke-
warm, but no one seemed to mind. The furniture was massive, leather-covered sofas and oak chairs surrounded the
fireplaces in two adjoining sitting rooms. Huge gilt-framed
landscapes of Scottish scenes adorned the walls. These I
studied carefully, having never seen real paintings on canvas,
let alone pictures of such unfamiliar highland sheep and
cattle. Scattered over the faded linoleum floors were Oriental
rugs. Things were well worn but clearly no one fretted over
polishing them the way my mother did. Before dinner,
everyone drank Scotch neat. Water was regarded as harmful
to the taste. Angus told me his parents had still toasted "the
king over the water" in his childhood, and that he remembered the rooms decorated with tartans. The woolshed was
massive, like the house and its contents. The shed was large
enough to shear what had once been a herd of forty thousand
sheep. Everything—quarters for station hands, stables, yards,
sheds for farm equipment—seemed on a gargantuan scale to
me, just as the vast paintings of highland landscapes seemed
to dwarf the people in the living rooms. I loved to hear Angus

tell stories about the pioneering days of his parents, and the way of life before railways and cars made such city comforts as store-bought canned goods accessible. Clare had experienced the same disasters as we had at Coorain, but ten lean years made little difference to the family fortune. On a station of this size, one could wait out the seasons with relative composure.

When the time came for us actually to pack for the train journey, I began to feel a strange emptiness in the pit of my stomach. My consciousness departed to some relatively distant point above my body, and I looked down at what seemed almost pygmy-size figures going about the business of departure. My mother, faced with a practical task, was her systematic self. Suitcases and trunks were packed. Boxes of china and linen, a few books, our clothes. But everything else remained, and I realized that we were going into the world outside relatively lighthanded. She broke down over the packing of my father's clothes. I, for my part, refused to pack any toys or dolls. I knew that in most important ways my childhood was over.

When the day of our departure dawned, it arrived as both a relief and a sentence. I wanted the break over, yet I could not bear to say good-bye. I was up and dressed early, uncomfortable in my town clothes. I took one last walk and found I had no heart for it. We drank the inevitable cup of morning tea as the bags and boxes were loaded. Suddenly, we were in the car driving away from Coorain. I looked back until it sank from sight beneath the horizon. My mother gazed resolutely ahead. In ten minutes it was all over.

Departures for Sydney by train took place at the small railroad station at Ivanhoe, some forty miles north of Coorain. There was little to the town but a cluster of railroad mainte-nance workers' huts, some shunting yards, and a set of stock-yards for loading sheep and cattle. A store, a garage, a road haulage company, and a few more ample houses lined the dusty main street. The train itself was the most impressive part of the landscape. The passenger train we rode on for half the journey to Sydney was one of our few chances to encounter modernity. It was diesel-powered, streamlined, air-conditioned, painted a dazzling silver to evoke the site of its origin, Broken Hill, an inland silver mining center. When the boys rode it to school, my father had always tipped the porter so that the boredom of their journey could be broken by an exciting ride in the engine cabin, actually watching the needle of the speedometer climb past eighty miles an hour. When the diesel engine had built up speed, it purred along effortlessly while the countryside outside raced by at a bewildering rate. The Diesel, as we called it, announced itself twenty or more minutes before its arrival by the huge column of red dust it churned up as it tore across the plains. We spent the twenty minutes in careful good-byes, and then piled quickly into the train which stopped only a merciful three minutes in the station. We both now wanted this ordeal over.

As the train pulled out and gathered speed, my mother and I stood at the door waving. We both choked with tears a little as we passed the system of points just outside the station where the train always slowed a little. Once my father, too preoccupied with giving advice to his sons to notice the time, had been obliged to jump from the moving train at that point.

Yet in counterpoint to my grief was overwhelming relief. It was true that we had been cast out from our paradise. But that paradise had become literally purgatorial for us. My mother had seen the product of fifteen years of unremitting labor disappear. She had lost a partnership of work and love which had made her utterly fulfilled. Without it she was at sea. I felt that my heart was permanently frozen with grief by what had happened to both my parents. I feared even greater disasters were we to remain at Coorain. I had lost my sense of trust in a benign providence, and feared the fates. My brother Bob had taken to reading me his favorite Shakespeare plays while home on his last vacation, and I had been transfixed by the line from *King Lear:* "As flies to wanton boys are we to the gods,/ They kill us for their sport." I did not understand the nature of the ecological disaster which had transformed my world, or that we ourselves had been agents as well as participants in our own catastrophe. I just knew that we had been defeated by the fury of the elements, a fury that I could not see we had earned. In the life that lay ahead, I knew I must serve as my father's agent in the family and muster the energy to deal with such further disasters as might befall us. For the moment, we were down on our luck and had to begin all over again.

from

THE LIARS' CLUB

MARY KARR

For all too many of us, coming of age is not a gentle process. We are pushed into greater knowing, very often against our will. In this excerpt from her searing memoir *The Liars' Club*, Mary Karr recalls the night when her emotionally unbalanced mother set her childhood on fire.

Grandma wound up leaving Mother a big pile of money, which didn't do us a lick of good, though Lord knows we needed it. Daddy's strike had dragged on till mid-March, pulling us way down in our bill-paying. He managed to keep up with the mortgage and utilities okay, but the grocery and drug bills and other sundries got out from under him. When he picked up his check at the paymaster's window on Fridays, he cashed it right there. Then he'd drive to Leechfield Pharmacy and go straight up to the pill counter in back to tell Mr. Juarez—kids called him Bugsy, after the cartoon bunny— that he'd come to pay at his bill. I can still see Daddy winking while he said it, *at*. He'd squint down at his billfold and lick his thumb and make a show of picking out a single crisp five-dollar bill and squaring it up on the counter between them. But that little "at" held back a whole tide of shame. It implied the bill weighed more than Daddy, superseded him in a way. In Jasper County, where he'd been raised, buying on credit was a sure sign of a man overreaching what he was. Even car loans were unheard-of, and folks were known to set down whole laundry sacks stuffed with one-dollar bills when it came time to pick up a new Jeep or tractor.

Bugsy knew these things. They mattered to him. He was a kind guy, prone to giving me comic books for free because it tickled him that I read so well. He always acted like he hated to take Daddy's money when it slid his way. "Heck, Pete. Put that back. We weren't a-waiting on this," he'd say, and Daddy would slide the bill closer and tell him to go on and take it. Then Bugsy would shrug out an okay. He'd ring some zeros up on the cash register and slip the bill into the right stack. He kept his accounts in a green book under the counter. He'd haul that out, find Daddy's name with his thick nicotine-stained finger, and note down the payment. Before we left, Bugsy usually led me to the back office, where he'd draw out his pocket knife to cut the binding cord on the new stack of funny books invariably standing in the corner. I'd sit on his desk and read out loud an entire issue of *Superman* or *Archie,* which skill caused him to smile into his coffee mug. Daddy would shake his head at this and say that I didn't need egging on because I had already gotten too big for my britches as it was.

That was the dance we went through with Bugsy on payday. The movements of it were both so exact and so fiercely casual that I never for a minute doubted that this whole money thing was, in fact, not casual at all, but serious as a stone. All the rest of the week, nobody talked about it. That silence slid over our house like a cold iron. But woe be it to you if you didn't finish your bowl of black-eyed peas, or if you failed to shut the icebox door flush so that it leaked cold and thereby ran up the electric. Daddy would come up behind you and shove that door all the way to or scoop the last peas into his own mouth with your very spoon. After doing so, he'd stare at you from the side of his face as if holding down a wealth of pissed-off over your evil wastefulness.

Evenings he wasn't working, he sat in bed to study his receipts and bills. He liked to spread out the old ones stamped PAID along the left side of the bedcovers. The new statements still in their envelopes ran along the right. He'd worked out a whole ritual to handle those bills. When one hit the mailbox, he slit it open, then marked down what he owed over the front address window where his name showed through. That way he sort of nodded at the debt right off, like he was saying *I know, I know.* Plus, he then didn't have to reopen and unfold every bill in order to worry over it. With all those envelopes staggered out in front of him, he drew hard on bottle after bottle of Lone Star beer and ciphered what he owed down the long margins of *The Leechfield Gazette,* all the time not saying boo about one dime of it.

I knew full well that people had way bigger problems than those Daddy had. Lots of guys didn't have jobs and houses at all. Or they had kids fall slobbering sick with leukemia, not to mention the umpteen-zillion people who were born in the Kalahari Desert or the streets of Calcutta blind or missing limbs or half-rotted-up as lepers. But Daddy's nightly cipherings were the most concentrated form of worry I've ever witnessed up close. That long line of numbers, done in his slanty, spidery scrawl, was not unlike the prayer that the penitent says over and over so that either the hope of that prayer or the full misery of what it's supposed to stave off will finally sink in.

Meanwhile, Mother was either laid up next to him slugging vodka from an aluminum green tumbler and reading, say, Leo Tolstoy (*Anna Karenina* was her favorite book) or else crying along with some Bessie Smith record. There was no more commerce between them than if a brick wall had run the length of that giant bed. Lecia and I tended to sprawl at the foot of it nights faking that we were doing the homework we both usually finished at school. We stayed there to keep an eye on all their worry, fearing it might somehow rise up above what they could handle and spill over us.

The mood in our house was tenser than when Grandma came to rot in the back bedroom. We'd gone back to our version of "normal." But our family habits seemed odder than ever, warped somehow by the judgment that Grandma's death implied and by Mother's sick, unspoken grief about it.

That spring Mother started walking around the house again buck naked. Daddy wore nothing but boxers, and Lecia and I alternately went flapping through the house either bare-assed when Daddy wasn't home, or wearing some combo of pajama tops and underpants (we called them *undersancies*) when he was. Don't get me wrong. We hadn't turned "naturist," though Mother did once shock the Leechfield PTA Mothers' Circle by claiming to have played volleyball on some nude beach in New Jersey. (That was the last time my school formally invited her anywhere; after that she occasionally gate-crashed the Christmas play, but otherwise was a vapor trail at school functions.) Lecia and I did earn nickels selling peeks at Mother's nudist cartoons from her *New Yorker* anthology. (We saved the art books for kids who could cough up as much as a quarter for a long stare at a Bosch painting with lots of skinny demons and some large-breasted matron being poked with sticks.)

Our staying undressed came from insomnia. As a family, we just couldn't sleep. From this state of constant, miserable exhaustion, we took up the hazy idea that sleep might come more often—it only arrived in spurts—if we were dressed for it, or, rather, undressed. Our bare bodies were walking invitations to any nap that might claim one of us. You could stagger into the living room most mornings and find one of our bodies sprawled asleep on the floorboards alongside the couch. Or you could come out at two a.m. and find Mother at the stove with her apron strings tied in a neat bow above her round butt as she worked on a Western omelet, while in the living room Lecia sat cross-legged in underpants slapping down cards for solitaire in front of the TV test pattern. We never came together in those hours, just wandered all over the house in various stages of neckedness.

In fact, the only time Mother got out of bed for any length of time that spring was to seal our windows off from the neighbors' view. One Sunday when I was hanging naked from the sturdy cast-iron rod over my window—Lecia and I were having a chin-up contest—I saw the Dillards' royal blue truck wheel slowly past carrying the whole gaggle of Dillards. They stared openmouthed at my hairless, dangling form. It startled me so I just hung there in full view a second, my nipples getting hard against the cold glass, before I got the wherewithal to drop from view. Then I crouched under the window ledge thinking how danged unfair it was: nobody on the block *ever* got up and out that early but us.

Mrs. Dillard and Fay were in the truck cab with their black mantillas on like they were heading to six a.m. mass. Even Junior and Joe had been stuck into white shirts with clip-on bow ties. They squatted on the flatbed's built-in toolbox. Their two blond heads were slicked flat with Butch Rose Wax. I could hear their laughing over the truck's rumbling muffler.

When Mother heard Lecia tease me about it in the kitchen, she decided to get out of bed. She threw the bedcovers off her legs, a gesture we'd all but deleted from our memory banks, and said it was a lot of horseshit caring if people saw you naked because we were all naked under our clothes anyway, but goddamn if she'd listen to me caterwaul about those boneheaded Dillards anymore. She was gonna seal over the windows so God Herself (she made a point of the female pronoun) couldn't see in.

Her method for this was wacky. First, she took a cheese grater and made crayon shavings in all different colors. She sprinkled these between sheets of wax paper and ironed the paper together till the crayon melted. With sable brushes and Elmer's glue, Lecia and I set to work pasting these squares of paper and color over all extant windows, an effect Mother likened to stained glass.

It was Mother's first enthusiasm in a long time, and we pounced on it. Lecia started racing with herself right off. She timed the process to see how fast she could paste over a whole window, then tried to beat that time.

Not long after we blanked out the windows, I came home from school and found the front door open and the screen ajar. That was weird, not only given our fierce need for privacy, but on account of all the roaches and june bugs, lizards and mosquitos down there. The semitropical climate could also send a spotty green-black mildew climbing your whitewashed walls if the full damp of the outdoors somehow got inside. You couldn't stop it entirely, but nobody left the door wide to it.

In my head, I go back to that open door. My penny loafers outside it are the color of oxblood and scuffed and run down on the inside from how pigeon-toed I am. I can almost feel the thump of my plaid book satchel on my right hip.

It was hot that day, the air thick as gauze. I bounded up the front steps after school having just gotten 100 on my spelling test. That grade barely beat out my class rival for the best grade, Peggy Fontenot, who'd lost two points for misspelling "said." I'd personally graded her paper, and my heart leapt up like a roe when I saw it spelled "sed." I had the winning test in my hand with the gold star that said my grade was highest. I raced up the concrete steps, even stopping short at the open screen before I slammed inside hollering I was home. I slung my book satchel over the sofa back and called again for Mother.

The silence that came back was even heavier than the air outside. It lay across the coarse rugs like swamp gas. Maybe that quiet somehow kick-started my fretting. Maybe then I paused to consider the oddness of that open door. I ran into the kitchen with the test still in hand looking to show it to Mother. There was only the black fan sweeping a dull little wind over a cup of cold coffee. No other sign. Back in the living room, I found the last page of the letter from Grandma's lawyer folded into about a dozen accordion pleats the way a kid would make a paper fan. Mother must have sat on the horsehair sofa using that fan to push a breeze across her face before dropping it there. I smoothed it out.

The oddest details from that letter have stayed with me, while other things—such as the exact amount of Mother's inheritance—have been sucked up into the void. Maybe the number was too large for my small skull to hold, being in the hundreds of thousands. (The figure also varies with Mother's telling, from "only $100,000" to "over half a million" depending on the point she's trying to make with the story. To this day, if pressed to give us the exact number, she presents a kind of walleyed expression with a loose-shouldered shrug that suggests such sums of money must be taken in stride, give or take a hundred thousand.) The stationery was thick and butter-colored. The page number was "6 of 6." The lawyer promised to wire $36,000—about four times what Daddy could make in a year before overtime—from the sale of Grandma's Lubbock house and farm to the Leechfield Bank, to thus-and-such an account number. We'd all expected that money. What this letter went on to describe that I didn't expect was the money from a new oil lease.

Apparently, Grandma hung on to the mineral rights for her land, keeping them in her name more from habit than any real hope of drilling oil there. Enough Dust Bowl crackers and dirt farmers out that way had sold their farms at fifty cents per acre one week only to watch a gusher spout all over the buyer's Cadillac the next for a faint dream of oil money to lie embedded in every West Texan's brainpan. You just did not sell mineral rights outright, ever. You held them. Even I knew that. You leased them for huge sums. (To my knowledge we still hold drilling rights on that land, though every inch of it has long since been proven bone-dry to the earth's core.) Anyway, it turned out that loads of would-be drillers had hounded Grandma for two decades to start poking holes in her stretch of desert. We never quite figured out her reasons for snubbing their offers. In one letter I found later, the old woman had explained to Mother that she was in the cotton business, not the petroleum business. Maybe she'd worried about getting bilked by some silver-tongued oil-company fellow, which bilking wouldn't befit her status as a prudent Methodist widow-lady and lifetime member of the Eastern Star. Somewhere in her effects, however, Mother's lawyer had found a letter from a Dallas oil baron. With Mother's permission, the lawyer would "execute an oil lease" for this guy. That was the exact phrase. I also recall moving my index finger along a string of five zeros, but I'm damned if I can conjure the exact amount the letter laid out. There was a lot of other stuff, of course, but I just remember my index finger stumping from one zero to the next. I counted till it hit me that we were in the hundred-thousand-dollar range, just one zero shy of the million mark, that magic number that sent dollar signs flying through movie montages. *Here,* I doubtless thought, *is the spotted pony I've run out looking for every Christmas morning. Here's a garnet birthstone ring from the baby Ferris wheel in Gibson's Jewelry.* And since I lacked for charity, I also probably had an idea like the following: *Maybe I can get to Disneyland and that lard-ass Peggy Fontenot can go screw.*

I ran through the house again then, calling out for Mother. What I found in her bathroom knocked the wind slap out of me. The big rectangular mirror over the sink had been scribbled up with lipstick of an orangey-red color. Somebody—Mother no doubt—had taken a tube of Mango Fandango or Kiss-Me Peach and scribbled that mirror almost solid, so the silver reflecting part came through only in streaks. In the sink there was a stub end of greasy lipstick. On the floor the empty gold tube lay like a spent shell casing on the fuzzy oval of yellow rug. I shied around it as I would a scorpion. A thin filter of fear came to slide between me and the world. Objects in the house started to get larger and more fluid. A standing lamp reared up at me as I came on it.

In Mother's bedroom, on the dresser mirror, I found the same lipstick scribbles done in hibiscus. The metal O of the tube had sawed through the silver surface. Other mirrors in other rooms held other lipstick colors—blue reds and mauves and pale titty-colored pinks, and that scary lipstick the color of muddy blood that Mother hardly ever wore because it made her look as pale and black-lipped as a silent-film star.

I went from mirror to scrawled-up mirror till I found the shattered one in our bathroom, which I imagined she'd gotten to last. A round smashed place in the center was about the diameter of her fist. Her face must have been floating in that exact spot when she broke it. The broken place itself was like a cyclone with whirled shatterings in the center and longer spikes radiating out. She must have watched the planes of her own angular face come apart like a cubist portrait. I backed away from the brokenness of it, giving the sink and the smatterings of glass on the floor wide berth.

I slammed outside and ran down the back steps, praying to God that the black spume of chimney smoke from the tin spout on the garage roof meant that I'd find Mother in her studio painting. If her car was missing, I knew I'd never see her again. I had no trouble picturing that car careening around a curve and then slamming into some concrete embankment. I could also see Mother slumped over the wheel with a picturesque trickle of blood coming from one ear. Surely she wanted to be stopped in her tracks that day. I prayed to find that car sitting in the garage, and I did; its headlights looked heavy-lidded and sleepy, like the car was some bored reptile squatting down over its own four tires.

The door from the garage to Mother's painting studio was open. The padlock was unlatched, and her silver key ring shaped like a longhorn steer and inlaid with turquoise still hung down from it. Mother sat in her mother's old rocker with her back to me. She was laying papers on a fire in the cast-iron stove. The white edges charred black and curled in. I knew not to speak. Above her on the wall, that big portrait of Grandma looked down, her stiff arms at perfect right angles. Mother had moved that portrait from the living room after the funeral, leaving the wall blank. It scared me to see Grandma Moore there gazing down at her.

There was a strange odor in the studio that day. On top of

the regular head-opening sting of turpentine and oil paints, I made out either lighter fluid or the charcoal starter Daddy always used to fire up the Weber grill. In fact, after I hit the doorway, Mother reached down for a can next to the rocker and squirted clear fluid from it so there was a whoosh. Flames licked out the stove front before settling back into their low rumble. (Later on, I'd find a brown scorch spot on the vaulted ceiling. I also later figured that she was feeding the stove with all the mail that had come addressed to Grandma since her death—bank statements and seed catalogues and get-well cards from the Lubbock Methodist Church Ladies' Auxiliary.)

Anyway, Mother's back to me in that rocker conjured that old Alfred Hitchcock movie *Psycho* she'd taken us to in 1960. In the end, the crazy killer was got up like his nutty old mother with a gray wig. He rocked in her personal chair. Mother turned around slow to face me like old Tony Perkins. Her face came into my head one sharp frame at a time. I finally saw in these instants that Mother's own face had been all scribbled up with that mud-colored lipstick. *She was trying to scrub herself out,* I thought. Sure enough, the scribbles weren't like those on an African mask or like a kid's war paint. They didn't involve the underlying face that much. They lacked form. No neat triangles or straight lines went along the planes on the face. She looked genuinely crazy sitting in her mother's rocker with the neatly ruffled blue calico cushions in front of that blazing stove with the smell of charcoal fluid and her own face all scrawled up bloody red.

Then we're in the lavender bedroom I share with Lecia. The sun is going down, so there's a vine pattern through the wax-papered windows, the shadows of wisteria and honeysuckle. Mother stands before this lit window over a cardboard box by our open closet. She picks up toys one at a time off the closet floor and flings them into the box. We have left our room a mess, she says in a hoarse voice I don't think of as hers. But that's the only voice she has left, her drunk Yankee one. *I want to be a good hausfrau,* she says, which word I didn't even know meant *housewife,* but I fear the hard German hiss of it. Hausfrau. *That's my job. That's what I am—the wife of this fucking crackerbox house.* And into the box fly the one-armed Barbies and fistfuls of checkers and marbles and plastic soldiers and metal cars and board games and the marble chess pieces—all hitting the cardboard with a sound like splattering rain.

Once the closet's bare, she yanks off our bedcovers and sails them through the room. She drags our mattress on the floor, then lifts our bare box spring over her head. She looks like Samson in Bible pictures with one of those big stone pillars bench-pressed up when she heaves it. It hits the wall with a deep-throated clang at once primitive and musical. That's what starts me crying for the only time that night. I duck my head and bury it in the armpit of Lecia's bleached white PJs.

Next I can see, we are out behind the garage in front of a

huge pile of toys and Golden Books and furniture heaped in a tall pyramid. I have been to football bonfires and beach-side pit barbecues with whole calves roasting on spits. Becky Hebert even once took me to a fish fry hosted by the Ku Klux Klan, where they were burning schoolbooks and drugstore romances in a pile higher than any of the houses around. This stack is almost as high as that. It's taller than Daddy, who's six feet in his socks.

I zero in on my old red wooden rocking horse. He stands not ten feet from me. He hangs all saggy now from his metal frame by these rusted springs. Mother is pouring gas out of the red can onto him, and he looks sullen underneath.

When she takes up the big box of safety matches, she waves Lecia and me back with a broad sweep of her arm, like she's about to do some circus trick. I start to stand so I can jump and catch her arm before she lights that match. But Lecia's hand clamps on both my shoulders to stop my rising. She shoves me back down onto the ground. I feel my legs buckle under me like they're the legs of some different girl, or even like the cold steel legs of one of those lawn chairs just folding up on itself. I sit down hard on the wet St. Augustine grass, the blades of which are stiff as plastic. That's my horse getting doused by the upended gas can. I knot my arms in front of my chest and think how I wanted to keep that horse for bouncing. It's supposed to be a baby toy, but some days when Lecia's out, I ride it with springs screeching and close my eyes and picture myself galloping across a wide prairie. Now that horse looks at me all blank-eyed and tired.

I scan around for a rock or two-by-four to conk Mother on the head with. But Lecia's hands won't let go my shoulders. She could be watching the weather on TV for all the feeling her face shows. I tell her that's my horse Mother's messing with. But she's bored with this complaint. So I let it go. *Bye-bye, old Paint,* I think to myself, *I'm a-leaving Cheyenne.*

Mother drags the safety match in slo-mo down the black strip on the side of the box, and the spark takes the red match head with a flare. She tosses the match toward the horse with a gesture that's almost delicate. For an instant she might be a lady dropping a hanky. Then flames surge up over my horse with a loud *whump.* For a long time inside the orange fire you can see the black horse shape real clear. But at some point that shape caves in on itself, gives way to the lapping fire that Mother pitches stuff into, no horse left at all. She upends the last box of toys and shakes it the way, earlier in our room, she dumped out each drawer from our highboy.

The fire is working hard. It climbs up and over every single object piled there. She's burning her own paintings too, some of them, the landscapes of the beach mostly. The canvases catch before the frames do, so lined up at different heights along one side of the pyramid are these framed pictures of flames. Fire burns wild inside the gilt frames and wormwood frames and slick, supermodern brass frames.

Then Mother drags across the grass the biggest, deepest box of all, an old refrigerator box we had been planning to cut up for a puppet theatre. Out of it she draws our clothes—culottes and sunsuits with shoulder ties and old pajamas with beading on the feet that make a clicking noise on the bathroom tiles and keep you from sliding around. A white shirt with a Peter Pan collar flies out of her hand and arcs across the black sky, and behind it comes a huge red crinoline petticoat I wore to can-can in. It always reminded Mother of Degas's dancers. Now it swirls from her hand in a circle and settles in the fire almost gently where it's eaten in a quick gulp. From Mother's arms tumble dozens of tennis shoes. They smother in a lump till the canvas of them catches, and after that, black smoke comes up with the wicked stink of scorched rubber.

After the shoes catch, she fishes out the dresses. She slips each one off its hanger the better to see it before she commends it to the fire. At her feet, a big thicket of hangers is piling up. Each hanger drops from her white hand into the pile with a faint ringing. That ringing sends her into heavy motion again. She holds every dress briefly by its shoulders like it's a schoolkid she's checking out for smudges before church. Then one by one they get flung away from her and into the fire. There sails my white eyelet-lace Easter dress, and the pinafore Grandma smocked and embroidered with French-knot flowers in pink. There's the pink peasant skirt

Lecia got at the Mexico store in Houston. There's the green plaid jumper with yellow cowgirl ropes stitched around the pockets that we've both worn. Those dresses look like nothing so much as the bodies of little girls whose ghosts have gone out of them. (Epictetus has a great line about the division between body and soul—"Thou art a little spirit bearing up a corpse." When I read that line years later, I automatically pictured those dresses emptied of their occupants and sailing into the fire in graceful arcs.)

At some point the fire fades to orange background, and I stare only at Mother's face. It's all streaked up with lipstick and soot, so she looks like a bona fide maniac. Her lips move in a muttery way, but I can't make out the words. Nipper growls and yaps. He occupies that large circle of dark by the house that barely exists for me anymore. I can hear him lunge to the end of his chain, then get his bark choked off by the collar before he slinks back under the house. Mother's voice rises, so I can make out what she's saying over the fire and the whimpering dog: *Rotten cocksucking motherfucking hausfrau.*

If I keep my eyes unfixed and look through my eyelashes I discover I can turn the whole night into something I drew with crayon. The trees around us have bubble-shaped heads. The dresses flying into the fire are cut out of a paper-doll book. The fire is burnt orange and sunflower yellow and fire-engine red, with bold black spikes around it. The refinery towers in the distance are long skinny lines I drew with the silver crayon, using my ruler to keep them so straight. Their fires remind me of birthday candles fixing to get puffed out.

I don't know when all the fight drains out of me, but it does. You could lead me by the hand straight into that fire, and I doubt a squawk would come out. I can't protest anymore, and I can see that Lecia has been scooped pretty empty too. We are in the grip of some big machine grinding us along. The force of it simplifies everything. A weird calm has settled over me from the inside out. What is about to happen to us has stood in line to happen. All the roads out of that instant have been closed, one and by one.

I think about the story of Job I heard in Carol Sharp's Sunday school. How he sort of learned to lean into feeling hurt at the end, the way you might lean into a heavy wind that almost winds up supporting you after a while. People can get behind pain that way, if they think it derives from powers larger than themselves. So in the middle of some miserable plague where everybody's got buboes in their groins and armpits swelling and bursting with pus, people can walk around calm. So I know with calm how cut off we are from any help. No fire truck will arrive. None of the neighbors will phone Daddy or the sheriff.

I picture old Mrs. Heinz standing next door at her sink behind the window she cleaned down to the squeak every Saturday with a bucket of ammonia water into which she squeezed a lemon. She can see us out there. I feel her eyes on me. She's wiping off the last plate from the drainboard and watching us and wondering should she come out. But she thinks better of it. Mother's flinging things into the fire like one of those witches out of the Shakespeare play, and old Mrs. Heinz probably peers out from behind the ruffled Priscilla curtains that she copied herself on her sewing machine using dimestore gingham to look like the ones in the Sears catalogue. She probably takes one long gander at that hill of flaming toys and furniture and the picture frames of living fire and Mother stirring it all with a long pole and thinks to herself, *Ain't a bit of my business.* Then she lets the pink-checked curtain go so it fell across us.

The other neighbors have done the same. I feel them all releasing us into the deep drop of whatever is about to happen. Each curtain falls. Each screen door is pulled tight, and every door hook clicks into its own tight eye, and even big heavy doors get heaved closed in the heat, and all the bolts are thrown. I can almost hear it happening all over the neighborhood. TVs get turned louder to shut out the racket of us. Anyone might have phoned Daddy and said, *Pete, looky here. This ain't none of my bi'ness, but . . .* (The thought that burdens me most today is that somebody did call Daddy to let him know, and Daddy—gripped by the same grinding machine that gripped us—just stayed in the slot that fate had carved for him and said he planned to come on home directly. Or he said kiss my rosy red ass, for Daddy could turn the volume on any portion of the world up or down when he had a mind to. I can very well picture his big hand setting the phone back in its black cradle. The men on his unit might have been frying up some catfish they'd caught. From high in his tower, he could have looked out that curved window across fields of industrial pipes and oil-storage tanks, past the train yards to the grid of identical houses—in the yard of one of which Mother was setting fire to our lives—and maybe Daddy just decided to change the channel away from that fire to the sizzle of cornbread-dipped catfish floating in hot lard. *Boy that fish smells good,* I can imagine him saying.)

When Mother gets done emptying stuff into the fire, she goes back inside the house, and we follow like herd animals. We don't run to some neighbor house calling, *save us save us.* We wouldn't leave Mother alone in this state. We cross the sopping lawn from the fire's scorch and into the humid damp of the dark yard and unlit house. We traipse up the concrete steps and into the kitchen at an even pace. She walks down the long hall to her bedroom, and at that moment, some spark of something must catch inside Lecia, some desire to get us both loose, to disembark from that wild ride we've been on, because she nudges me to our end of the house. I go where she pushes like a blind calf.

Our room is scrambled and holds no order. That box spring tilting against the wall scares me big league. I can picture Mother heaving it and hear it hit all over again. There's a gray-and-black quilt Grandma once stitched together from a book of men's suit samples she got from some tailor. Lecia spreads that out like we're on a picnic. I lie down on it, and she draws the white chenille bedspread over our knees, which we bend into mountains. The chenille is nubbly as code. We roll on our sides and face each other. The quilt squares stretch beneath us. We hopscotch from square to square in finger tag—black gabardine to charcoal flannel to gray pinstripe, like farmlands seen from up high. Mother earlier smashed all the lightbulbs in our room with a broom handle, so it's dark. You can't quite decipher the individual pieces of furniture tipped over and flung around, just the right angles that poke up making a jagged mountain landscape around our floor pallet.

I can hear Mother in the kitchen now. She must be dumping cutlery from the drawers because the noise of metal crashing explodes then stops, explodes then stops. If I close my eyes it's like a great battle right out of King Arthur is taking place in there. I can picture knights in armor bringing their swords down against shields, arrows flying into battlements, lances striking the breastplates of horsemen. When I open my eyes, though, there is only the dark plain of the quilt we lie on divided up in squares by the neat grid of suit samples. Next to me Lecia's face is long and white under her spiky bangs. She looks baleful as a basset hound. She has stopped hopscotching and now presses her index finger against her lips to show me not to say anything, but what might I say? A long rectangle of light spills over us from the open door.

Then a dark shape comes to occupy that light, a figure in the shape of my mom with a wild corona of hair and no face but a shadow. She has lifted her arms and broadened the stance of her feet, so her shadow turns from a long thin line into a giant X. And swooping down from one hand is the twelve-inch shine of a butcher knife, not unlike the knife that crazy guy had in *Psycho* for the shower scene, a stretched-out triangle of knife that Daddy sharpens by hand on his whetstone before he dismantles a squirrel or a chicken, though it is also big enough to have hacked through the hip joint of a buck. It holds a glint of light on its point like a star, so that old rhyme pops into my head: *Star light, star bright, first star I see tonight. I wish I may, I wish I might, have the wish I wish tonight.* Then I don't know what to wish for. Lecia's finger stays pressed to her lips. Her eyes are big but steady on that figure in the doorway and on the knife. I wish not to scream. Screaming would piss Lecia off. I can tell. A scream is definitely not what I want to happen to me right now. It's part wish and part prayer that zips through my head and keeps me from howling.

No sooner do I choke down that scream than a miracle happens. A very large pool of quiet in my head starts to spread. Lecia's face shrinks back like somebody in the wrong end of your telescope. Then even Mother's figure starts to alter and fade. In fact, the thin, spidery female form in black stretch pants and turtleneck wielding a knife in one upraised arm is only a stick figure of my mother, like the picture I drew in Magic Marker on the Mother's Day card I gave her last Sunday. I wrote underneath it in pink block letters that I decorated with crayon drawings of lace, "You are a nice Mom. I love you. It has been nice with you. Love from Mary Marlene." That Sunday morning when she'd opened that card up and read it, she cried racking sobs and hugged me hard so her tears streamed down into my ears till Lecia showed up at Mother's bedside with a vodka martini she'd mixed saying, *Here, sip at this.* Then there was another martini and another. Della Reese was singing "Mack the Knife" on the record player. She kept saying *My poor, poor babies* and *This isn't your fault.* By the time I got my nerve up to sneak in the kitchen and upend the vodka bottle down the sink, there was only an inch left anyway.

That was Mother's Day a week ago. On my card, I had drawn a stick-figure mom wearing a string of Ping-Pong–sized pearls around its stick neck. Now in my mind, that stick figure is what Mother becomes. She's just a head like a ball and curly scribbles for hair. But there the likeness to the figure on my card ends. This stick figure holds a triangle knife with a star glinting off its end. My stick-figure sister is breathing deep in the chest of her white PJs, and I match my breath to hers. We lie there in that cartoon of a room for what seems like forever, and then out of nowhere Mother roars *No!* like a lioness, her mouth shapes itself into a giant black O with real definite pointy teeth for what seems like a long time. The black *NO* sails out of that mouth in a long balloon with the tail of a comet streaking past us and out the wax-papered windows into the flaming night.

That's how God answered my prayers: I learned to make us all into cartoons. That stick woman in the center of the big black page with her eyebrows squinched down in a mad V over pin-dot eyes is no more my mother than some monster on the Saturday cartoons. She just isn't. I lock all my scared-ness down in my stomach until the fear hardens into something I hardly notice. I myself harden into a person that I hardly notice. I can feel Lecia cock her head at me, like she wants to know what the hell I have to grin about.

Now the stick-figure mom sets down the knife on the floor to dial the phone. I count the seven turns of the dial, feel it unwind under her stick finger. She's crying, the stick mommy, with sucking sobs. A whole fountain of blue tears pours from both pin-dot eyes. I guess it's Dr. Boudreaux who answers on the other end, because she says, "Forest, it's Charlie Marie. Get over here. I just killed them both. Both of them. I've stabbed them both to death."

from

GRENDEL

JOHN GARDNER

The world can be a scary place, our first solo steps into it sometimes traumatic. Though the Grendel of John Gardner's imaginative retelling of *Beowulf* does not enjoy what we might call a typical childhood, his violent awakening to the state of things outside his cave and inside his mind can stand for the youthful experiences of many.

Talking, talking, spinning a spell, pale skin of words that closes me in like a coffin. Not in a language that anyone any longer understands. Rushing, degenerate mutter of noises I send out before me wherever I creep, like a dragon burning his way through vines and fog.

I used to play games when I was young—it might as well be a thousand years ago. Explored our far-flung underground world in an endless wargame of leaps onto nothing, ingenious twists into freedom or new perplexity, quick whispered plottings with invisible friends, wild cackles when vengeance was mine. I nosed out, in my childish games, every last shark-toothed chamber and hall, every black tentacle of my mother's cave, and so came at last, adventure by adventure, to the pool of firesnakes. I stared, mouth gaping. They were gray as old ashes; faceless, eyeless. They spread the surface of the water with pure green flame. I knew—I seemed to have known all along—that the snakes were there to guard something. Inevitably, after I'd stood there a while, rolling my eyes back along the dark hallway, my ears cocked for my mother's step, I screwed my nerve up and dove. The firesnakes scattered as if my flesh were charmed. And so I discovered the sunken door, and so I came up, for the first time, to moonlight.

I went no farther, that first night. But I came out again,

inevitably. I played my way farther out into the world, vast cavern aboveground, cautiously darting from tree to tree challenging the terrible forces of night on tiptoe. At dawn I fled back.

I lived those years, as do all young things, in a spell. Like a puppy nipping, playfully growling preparing for battle with wolves. At times the spell would be broken suddenly: on shelves or in hallways of my mother's cave, large old shapes with smouldering eyes sat watching me. A continuous grumble came out of their mouths; their backs were humped. Then little by little it dawned on me that the eyes that seemed to bore into my body were in fact gazing through it, wearily indifferent to my slight obstruction of the darkness. Of all the creatures I knew, in those days, only my mother really looked at me.—Stared at me as if to consume me, like a troll. She loved me, in some mysterious sense I understood without her speaking it. I was her creation. We were one thing, like the wall and the rock growing out from it.—Or so I ardently, desperately affirmed. When her strange eyes burned into me, it did not seem quite sure. I was intensely aware of when I sat, the volume of darkness I displaced, the shiny-smooth span of packed dirt between us, and the shocking separateness from me in my mama's eyes. I would feel, all at once, alone and ugly, almost—as if I'd dirtied myself—obscene. The cavern river rumbled far below us. Being young, unable to face these things, I would bawl and hurl myself at my mother and she would reach out her claws and seize me, though I could see I alarmed her (I had teeth like a saw), and she would smash me to her fat, limp breast as if to make me a part of her flesh again. After that, comforted, I would gradually ease back out into my games. Crafty-eyed, wicked as an elderly wolf, I would scheme with or stalk my imaginary friends, projecting the self I meant to become into every dark corner of the cave and the woods above.

Then all at once there they'd be again, the indifferent, burning eyes of the strangers. Or my mother's eyes. Again my world would be suddenly transformed, fixed like a rose with a nail through it, space hurtling coldly out from me in all directions. But I didn't understand.

One morning I caught my foot in the crack where two old treetrunks joined. "Owp!" I yelled. "Mama! Waa!" I was out much later than I'd meant to be. As a rule I was back in the cave by dawn, but that day I'd been lured out farther than usual by the heavenly scent of newborn calf—ah, sweeter than flowers, as sweet as my mama's milk. I looked at the foot in anger and disbelief. It was wedged deep, as if the two oak trees were eating it. Black sawdust—squirreldust—was spattered up the leg almost to the thigh. I'm not sure now how the accident happened. I must have pushed the two boles apart as I stepped up into the place where they joined, and then when I stupidly let go again they closed on my foot like a trap. Blood gushed from my ankle and shin, and pain flew up through me like fire up the flue of a mountain. I lost my head. I bellowed for help, so loudly it made the ground shake, "Mama! Waa! Waaa!" I bellowed to the sky, the forest, the cliffs, until I was so weak from loss of blood I could barely wave my arms. "I'm going to die," I wailed. "Poor Grendel! Poor old Mama! I wept and sobbed. Poor Grendel will hang here and starve to death," I told myself, "and no one will ever even miss him!" The thought enraged me. I hooted. I thought of my mother's foreign eyes, staring at me from across the room: I thought of the cool, indifferent eyes of the others. I shrieked in fear; still no one came.

The sun was up now, and even filtered as it was through the lacy young leaves, it made my head hurt. I twisted around as far as I could, hunting wildly for her shape on the cliffs, but there was nothing, or, rather, there was everything but my mother. Thing after thing tried, cynical and cruel, to foist itself off as my mama's shape—a black rock balanced at the edge of the cliff, a dead tree casting a long-armed shadow, a running stag, a cave entrance—each thing trying to detach itself, lift itself out of the general meaningless scramble of objects, but falling back, melting to the blank, infuriating clutter of not-my-mother. My heart began to race. I seemed to see the whole universe, even the sun and sky, leaping forward, then sinking away again, decomposing. Everything was wreckage, putrefaction. If she were there, the cliffs, the brightening sky, the trees, the stag, the waterfall would sud-

denly snap into position around her, sane again, well organized; but she was not, and the morning was crazy. Its green
brilliance jabbed at me, live needles.

"Please, Mama!" I sobbed as if heartbroken.

Then, some thirty feet away, there was a bull. He stood
looking at me with his head lowererd, and the world snapped
into position around him, as if in league with him. I must
have been closer to the calf than I had guessed, since he'd
arrived to protect it. Bulls do such things, though they don't
even know that the calves they defend are theirs. He shook
his horns at me, as if scornful. I trembled. On the ground, on
two good feet, I would have been more than a match for the
bull, or if not, I could have outrun him. But I was four or five
feet up in the air, trapped and weak. He could slam me right
out of the tree with one blow of that boned, square head,
maybe tearing the foot off, and then he could gore me to
death at his leisure in the grass. He pawed the ground,
looking at me up-from-under, murderous. "Go away!" I said.
"Hssst!" It had no effect. I bellowed at him. He jerked his
head as if the sound were a boulder I'd thrown at him, but
then he merely stood considering, and, after a minute, he
pawed the ground again. Again I bellowed. This time he
hardly noticed it. He snorted through his nose and pawed
more deeply, spattering grass and black earth at his sharp rear
hooves. As if time had slowed down as it does for the dying,
I watched him loll his weight forward, sliding into an easy

lope, head tilted, coming toward me in a casual arc. He picked up speed, throwing his weight onto his huge front shoulders, crooked tail lifted behind him like a flag. When I screamed, he didn't even flick an ear but came on, driving like an avalanche now, thunder booming from his hooves across the cliffs. The same instant he struck my tree he jerked his head and flame shot up my leg. The tip of one horn had torn me to the knee.

But that was all. The tree shuddered as he banged it with his skull, and he pivoted around it, stumbling. He gave his head a jerk, as if clearing his brains, then turned and loped back to where he'd charged me from before. He'd struck too low, and even in my terror I understood that he would always strike too low: he fought by instinct, blind mechanism ages old. He'd have fought the same way against an earthquake or an eagle: I had nothing to fear from his wrath but that twisting horn. The next time he charged I kept my eye on it, watched that horn with as much concentration as I'd have watched the rims of a crevasse I was leaping, and at just the right instant I flinched. Nothing touched me but the breeze as the horn flipped past.

I laughed. My ankle was numb now; my leg was on fire to the hip. I twisted to search the cliffwalls again, but still my mother wasn't there, and my laughter grew fierce. All at once, as if by sudden vision, I understood the emptiness in the eyes of those humpbacked shapes back in the cave. (Were they my brothers, my uncles, those creatures shuffling brimstone-eyed from room to room, or sitting separate, isolated, muttering forever like underground rivers, each in his private, inviolable gloom?)

I understood that the world was nothing: a mechanical chaos of casual, brute enmity on which we stupidly impose our hopes and fears. I understood that, finally and absolutely, I alone exist. All the rest, I saw, is merely what pushes me, or what I push against, blindly—as blindly as all that is not myself pushes back. I create the whole universe, blink by blink.—An ugly god pitifully dying in a tree!

The bull struck again. I flinched from the horntip and bellowed with rage and pain. The limbs overhead, stretching out through the clearing like hungry snakes reaching up from their nest, would be clubs if I had them in my two hands, or barricades, piled between me and my cave, or kindling down in the room where my mother and I slept. Where they were, above me, they were—what? Kind shade? I laughed. A tearful howl.

The bull kept on charging. Sometimes after he hit he'd fall down and lie panting. I grew limp with my anarchistic laughter. I no longer bothered to jerk back my leg. Sometimes the horntip tore it, sometimes not. I clung to the treetrunk that slanted off to my right, and I almost slept. Perhaps I did sleep, I don't know. I must have. Nothing mattered. Sometime in the middle of the afternoon I opened my eyes and discovered that the bull was gone.

I slept again, I think. When I woke up this time and looked up through the leaves overhead, there were vultures. I sighed, indifferent. I was growing used to the pain, or it had lessened. Unimportant. I tried to see myself from the vultures' viewpoint. I saw, instead, my mother's eyes. Consuming. I was suddenly her focus of the general meaninglessness—not for myself, not for any quality of my large, shaggy body or my sly, unnatural mind. I was, in her eyes, some meaning I myself could never know and might not care to know: an alien, the rock broken free of the wall. I slept again.

That night, for the first time, I saw men.

It was dark when I awakened—or when I came to, if it was that. I was aware at once that there was something wrong. There was no sound, not even the honk of a frog or the chirp of a cricket. There was a smell, a fire very different from ours, pungent, painful as thistles to the nose. I opened my eyes and everything was blurry, as though underwater. There were lights all around me, like some weird creature's eyes. They jerked back as I looked. Then voices, speaking words. The sounds foreign at first, but when I calmed myself, concentrating, I found I understood them: it was my own language, but spoken in a strange way, as if the sounds were made by brittle sticks, dried spindles, flaking bits of shale. My vision cleared and I saw them, mounted on horses, holding torches up. Some of them had shiny domes (as it seemed to me then) with horns coming out, like the bull's.

They were small, these creatures, with dead-looking eyes and gray-white faces, and yet in some ways they were like us, except ridiculous and, at the same time, mysteriously irritating, like rats. Their movements were stiff and regular, as if figured by logic. They had skinny, naked hands that moved by clicks. When I first became aware of them, they were all speaking at the same time. I tried to move, but my body was rigid; only one hand gave a jerk. They all stopped speaking at the same instant, like sparrows. We stared at each other.

One of them said—a tall one with a long black beard—"It moves independent of the tree."

They nodded.

The tall one said, "It's a growth of some kind, that's my opinion. Some beastlike fungus."

They all looked up into the branches.

A short, fat one with a tangled white beard pointed up into the tree with an ax. "Those branches on the northern side are all dead there. No doubt the whole tree'll be dead before midsummer. It's always the north side goes first when there ain't enough sap."

They nodded, an another one said, "See there where it grows up out of the trunk? Sap running all over."

They leaned over the sides of their horses to look, pushing the torches toward me. The horses' eyes glittered.

"Have to close that up if we're going to save this tree," the tall one said. The others grunted, and the tall one looked up at my eyes, uneasy. I couldn't move. He stepped down off the horse and came over to me, so close I could have swung my hand and smashed his head if I could make my muscles move. "It's like blood," he said, and made a face.

Two of the others got down and came over to pull at their noses and look.

"I say that tree's a goner," one of them said.

They all nodded, except the tall one. "We can't just leave it rot," he said. "Start letting the place go to ruin and you know what the upshot'll be."

They nodded. The others got down off their horses and came over. The one with the tangled white beard said, "Maybe we could chop the fungus out."

They thought about it. After a while the tall one shook his head. "I don't know. Could be it's some kind of a oaktree spirit. Better not to mess with it."

They looked uneasy. There was a hairless, skinny one with eyes like two holes. He stood with his arms out, like a challenged bird, and he kept moving around in jerky little circles, bent forward, peering at everything, at the tree, at the woods around, up into my eyes. Now suddenly he nodded. "That's it! King's right! It's a spirit!"

"You think so?" they said. Their hands poked forward.

"Sure of it," he said.

"Is it friendly, you think?" the king said.

The hairless one peered up at me with the fingertips of

one hand in his mouth. The skinny elbow hung straight down, as if he were leaning on an invisible table while he thought the whole thing through. His black little eyes stared straight into mine, as if waiting for me to tell him something. I tried to speak. My mouth moved, but nothing would come out. The little man jerked back. "He's hungry!" he said.

"Hungry!" they all said. "What does he eat?"

He looked at me again. His tiny eyes drilled into me and he was crouched as if he were thinking of trying to jump up into my brains. My heart thudded. I was so hungry I could eat a rock. He smiled suddenly, as if a holy vision had exploded in his head. "He eats *pig!*" he said. He looked doubtful. "Or maybe pigsmoke. He's in a period of transition."

They all looked at me, thinking it over, then nodded.

The king picked out six men. "Go get the thing some pigs," he said. The six men said "Yes sir!" and got on their horses and rode off. It filled me with joy, though it was all crazy, and before I knew I could do it, I laughed. They jerked away and stood shaking, looking up.

"The spirit's angry," one of them whispered.

"It always has been," another one said. "That's why it's killing the tree."

"No, no, you're wrong," the hairless one said. "It's yelling for pig."

"Pig!" I tried to yell. It scared them.

They all began shouting at each other. One of the horses

neighed and reared up, and for some crazy reason they took it for a sign. The king snatched an ax from the man beside him and, without any warning, he hurled it at me. I twisted, letting out a howl, and it shot past my shoulder, just barely touching my skin. Blood trickled out.

"You're all crazy," I tried to yell, but it came out a moan. I bellowed for my mother.

"Surround him!" the king yelled, "Save the horses!"—and suddenly I knew I was dealing with no dull mechanical bull but with thinking creatures, pattern makers, the most dangerous things I'd ever met. I shrieked at them, trying to scare them off, but they merely ducked behind bushes and took long sticks from the saddles of their horses, bows and javelins. "You're all crazy," I bellowed, "you're all insane!" I'd never howled more loudly in my life. Darts like hot coals went through my legs and arms and I howled more loudly still. And then, just when I was sure I was finished, a shriek ten times as loud as mine came blaring off the cliff. It was my mother! She came roaring down like thunder, screaming like a thousand hurricanes, eyes as bright as dragonfire, and before she was within a mile of us, the creatures had leaped to their horses and galloped away. Big trees shattered and fell from her path; the earth trembled. Then her smell poured in like blood into a silver cup, filling the moonlit clearing to the brim, and I felt the two trees that held me falling, and I was tumbling, free, into the grass.

I woke up in the cave, warm firelight flickering on walls. My mother lay picking through the bone pile. When she heard me stir, she turned, wrinkling her forehead, and looked at me. There were no other shapes. I think I dimly understood even then that they'd gone deeper into darkness, away from men. I tried to tell her all that had happened, all that I'd come to understand: the meaningless objectness of the world, the universal bruteness. She only stared, troubled at my noise. She'd forgotten all language long ago, or maybe had never known any. I'd never heard her speak to the other shapes. (How I myself learned to speak I can't remember; it was a long, long time ago.) But I talked on, trying to smash through the walls of her unconsciousness. "The world resists me and I resist the world," I said. "That's all there is. The mountains are what I define them as." Ah, monstrous stupidity of childhood, unreasonable hope! I waken with a start and see it over again (in my cave, out walking, or sitting by the mere), the memory rising as if it has been pursuing me. The fire in my mother's eyes brightens and she reaches out as if some current is tearing us apart. "The world is all pointless accident," I say. Shouting now, my fists clenched. "I exist, nothing else." Her face works. She gets up on all fours, brushing dry bits of bone from her path, and, with a look of terror, rising as if by unnatural power, she hurls herself across the void and buries me in her bristly fur and fat. I sicken with fear. "My mother's fur is bristly," I say to myself. "Her flesh is loose." Buried under my mother I cannot see. She smells of wild pig and fish. "My mother smells of wild pig and fish," I say. What I see I inspire with useful-ness, I think, trying to suck in breath, and all that I do not see is useless, void. I observe myself observing what I observe. It startles me. "Then I am not that which observes!" I am *lack*. *Alack!* No thread, no frailest hair between myself and the uni-versal clutter! I listen to the underground river. I have never seen it.

Talking, talking, spinning a skin, a skin . . .

I can't breathe, and I claw to get free. She struggles. I smell my mama's blood and, alarmed, I hear from the walls and floor of the cave the booming, booming, of her heart.

from

A MAN CALLED WHITE

WALTER WHITE

Until he was 12, blonde-haired, blue-eyed Walter
White identified himself as African American only in
name. But when a race riot in Atlanta brought a
white mob to the door of his family home, White
suddenly acquired a profound knowledge of
who he was, a knowledge that would eventually
allow him to lead the NAACP.

I am a Negro. My skin is white, my eyes are blue, my hair is blond. The traits of my race are nowhere visible upon me. Not long ago I stood one morning on a subway platform in Harlem. As the train came in I stepped back for safety. My heel came down upon the toe of the man behind me. I turned to apologize to him. He was a Negro, and his face as he stared at me was hard and full of the piled-up bitterness of a thousand lynchings and a million nights in shacks and tenements and "nigger towns." "Why don't you look where you're going?" he said sullenly. "You white folks are always trampling on colored people." Just then one of my friends came up and asked how the fight had gone in Washington—there was a filibuster against legislation for a permanent Fair Employment Practices Committee. The Negro on whose toes I had stepped listened, then spoke to me penitently:

"Are you Walter White of the NAACP? I'm sorry I spoke to you that way. I thought you were white."

I am not white. There is nothing within my mind and heart which tempts me to think I am. Yet I realize acutely that the only characteristic which matters to either the white or the colored race—the appearance of whiteness—is mine. There is magic in a white skin; there is tragedy, loneliness, exile, in a black skin. Why then do I insist that I am a Negro, when nothing compels me to do so but myself?

Many Negroes are judged as whites. Every year approximately twelve thousand white-skinned Negroes disappear—people whose absence cannot be explained by death or emigration. Nearly every one of the fourteen million discernible Negroes in the United States knows at least one member of his race who is "passing"—the magic word which means that some Negroes can get by as whites, men and women who have decided that they will be happier and more successful if they flee from the proscription and humiliation which the American color line imposes on them. Often these emigrants achieve success in business, the professions, the arts and sciences. Many of them have married white people, lived happily with them, and produced families. Sometimes they tell their husbands or wives of their Negro blood, sometimes not. Who are they? Mostly people of no great importance, but some of them prominent figures, including a few members of Congress, certain writers, and several organizers of movements to "keep the Negroes and other minorities in their places." Some of the most vehement public haters of Negroes are themselves secretly Negroes.

They do not present openly the paradox of the color line. It is I, with my insistence, day after day, year in and year out, that I am a Negro, who provoke the reactions to which now I am accustomed: the sudden intake of breath, the bewildered expression of the face, the confusion of the eyes, the muddled fragmentary remarks—"But you do not look . . . I mean I would never have known . . . of course if you didn't want to admit . . ." Sometimes the eyes blink rapidly and the tongue, out of control, says, "Are you sure?"

I have tried to imagine what it is like to have me presented to a white person as a Negro, by supposing a Negro were suddenly to say to me, "I am white." But the reversal does not work, for whites can see no reason for a white man ever wanting to be black; there is only reason for a black man wanting to be white. That is the way whites think; that is the way their values are set up. It is the startling removal of the blackness that upsets people. Looking at me without knowing who I am, they disassociate me from all the characteristics of the Negro. Informed that I am a Negro, they find it impossible suddenly to endow me with the skin, the odor, the dialect, the shuffle, the imbecile good nature, traditionally attributed to Negroes. Instantly they are aware that these things are *not* part of me. They think there must be some mistake.

There is no mistake. I am a Negro. There can be no doubt. I know the night when, in terror and bitterness of soul, I discovered that I was set apart by the pigmentation of my skin (invisible though it was in my case) and the moment at which I decided that I would infinitely rather be what I was than, through taking advantage of the way of escape that was open to me, be one of the race which had forced the decision upon me.

There were nine light-skinned Negroes in my family:

mother, father, five sisters, an older brother, George, and myself. The house in which I discovered what it meant to be a Negro was located on Houston Street, three blocks from the Candler Building, Atlanta's first skyscraper, which bore the name of the ex–drug clerk who had become a millionaire from the sale of Coca-Cola. Below us lived none but Negroes; toward town all but a very few were white. Ours was an eight room, two-story frame house which stood out in its surroundings not because of its opulence but by contrast with the drabness and unpaintedness of the other dwellings in a deteriorating neighborhood.

Only Father kept his house painted, the picket fence repaired, the board fence separating our place from those on either side white-washed, the grass neatly trimmed, and flower beds abloom. Mother's passion for neatness was even more pronounced and it seemed to me that I was always the victim of her determination to see no single blade of grass longer than the others or any one of the pickets in the front fence less shiny with paint than its mates. This spic-and-spanness became increasingly apparent as the rest of the neighborhood became more down-at-heel, and resulted, as we were to learn, in sullen envy among some of our white neighbors. It was the violent expression of that resentment against a Negro family neater than themselves which set the pattern of our lives.

On a day in September 1906, when I was thirteen, we

were taught that there is no isolation from life. The unseasonably oppressive heat of an Indian summer day hung like a steaming blanket over Atlanta. My sisters and I had casually commented upon the unusual quietness. It seemed to stay Mother's volubility and reduced Father, who was more taciturn, to monosyllables. But, as I remember it, no other sense of impending trouble impinged upon our consciousness.

I had read the inflammatory headlines in the *Atlanta News* and the more restrained ones in the *Atlanta Constitution* which reported alleged rapes and other crimes committed by Negroes. But these were so standard and familiar that they made—as I look back on it now—little impression. The stories were more frequent, however, and consisted of eight-column streamers instead of the usual two- or four-column ones.

Father was a mail collector. His tour of duty was from three to eleven p.m. He made his rounds in a little cart into which one climbed from a step in the rear. I used to drive the cart for him from two until seven, leaving him at the point nearest our home on Houston Street, to return home either for study or sleep. That day Father decided that I should not go with him. I appealed to Mother, who thought it might be all right, provided Father sent me home before dark because, she said, "I don't think they would dare start anything before nightfall." Father told me as we made the rounds that ominous rumors of a race riot that night were sweeping the town.

But I was too young that morning to understand the background of the riot. I became much older during the next thirty-six hours, under circumstances which I now recognize as the inevitable outcome of what had preceded.

One of the most bitter political campaigns of that bloody era was reaching its climax. Hoke Smith—that amazing contradiction of courageous and intelligent opposition to the South's economic ills and at the same time advocacy of ruthless suppression of the Negro—was a candidate that year for the governorship. His opponent was Clark Howell, editor of the *Atlanta Constitution*, which boasted with justification that it "covers Dixie like the dew." Howell and his supporters held firm authority over the state Democratic machine despite the long and bitter fight Hoke Smith had made on Howell in the columns of the rival *Atlanta Journal*.

Hoke Smith had fought for legislation to ban child labor and railroad rate discriminations. He had denounced the corrupt practices of the railroads and the state railway commission, which, he charged, was as much owned and run by northern absentee landlords as were the railroads themselves. He had fought for direct primaries to nominate senators and other candidates by popular vote, for a corrupt practices act, for an elective railway commission, and for state ownership of railroads—issues which were destined to be still fought for nearly four decades later by Ellis Arnall. For these reforms he was hailed throughout the nation as a genuine progressive along with La Follette of Wisconsin and Folk of Missouri.

To overcome the power of the regular Democratic organization, Hoke Smith sought to heal the feud of long standing between himself and the powerful ex-radical Populist, Thomas E. Watson. Tom Watson was the strangest mixture of contradictions which rotten-borough politics of the South had ever produced. He was the brilliant leader of an agrarian movement in the South which, in alliance with the agrarian West, threatened for a time the industrial and financial power of the East. He had made fantastic strides in uniting Negro and white farmers with Negro and white industrial workers. He had advocated enfranchisement of Negroes and poor whites, the abolition of lynching, control of big business, and rights for the little man, which even today would label him in the minds of conservatives as a dangerous radical. He had fought with fists, guns, and spine-stirring oratory in a futile battle to stop the spread of an industrialized, corporate society.

His break with the Democratic Party during the '90s and the organization of the Populist Party made the Democrats his implacable enemies. The North, busy building vast corporations and individual fortunes, was equally fearful of Tom Watson. Thus was formed between reactionary Southern Democracy and conservative Northern Republicanism the basis of cooperation whose fullest flower is to be seen in the present-day coalition of conservatives in Congress. This combination crushed Tom Watson's bid for national leadership in the presidential elections of 1896 and smashed the Populist movement. Watson ran for president in 1904 and 1908, both times with abysmal failure. His defeats soured him to the point of vicious acrimony. He turned from his ideal of interracial decency to one of virulent hatred and denunciation of the "nigger." He thus became a natural ally for Hoke Smith in the gubernatorial election in Georgia in 1906.

The two rabble-rousers stumped the state screaming, "Nigger, nigger, nigger!" Some white farmers still believed Watson's abandoned doctrine that the interests of Negro and white farmers and industrial workers were identical. They feared that Watson's and Smith's new scheme to disfranchise Negro voters would lead to disfranchisement of poor whites. Tom Watson was sent to trade on his past reputation to reassure them that such was not the case and that their own interests were best served by now hating "niggers."

Watson's oratory had been especially effective among the cotton mill workers and other poor whites in and near Atlanta. The *Atlanta Journal* on August 1, 1906, in heavy type, all capital letters, printed an incendiary appeal to race prejudice backing up Watson and Smith which declared:

> Political equality being thus preached to the
> negro in the ring papers and on the stump, what

wonder that he makes no distinction between political and social equality? He grows more bumptious on the street, more impudent in his dealings with white men, and then, when he cannot achieve social equality as he wishes, with the instinct of the barbarian to destroy what he cannot attain to, he lies in wait, as that dastardly brute did yesterday near this city, and assaults the fair young girlhood of the south . . .

At the same time, a daily newspaper was attempting to wrest from the *Atlanta Journal* leadership in the afternoon field. The new paper, the *Atlanta News*, in its scramble for circulation and advertising took a lesson from the political race and began to play up in eight-column streamers stories of the raping of white women by Negroes. That every one of the stories was afterward found to be wholly without foundation was of no importance. The *News* circulation, particularly in street sales, leaped swiftly upward as the headlines were bawled by lusty-voiced newsboys. Atlanta became a tinder box.

Fuel was added to the fire by a dramatization of Thomas Dixon's novel *The Clansman* in Atlanta. (This was later made by David Wark Griffith into *The Birth of a Nation,* and did more than anything else to make successful the revival of the Ku Klux Klan.) The late Ray Stannard Baker, telling the story of the Atlanta riot in *Along the Color Line,* characterized

Dixon's fiction and its effect on Atlanta and the South as "incendiary and cruel." No more apt or accurate description could have been chosen.

During the afternoon preceding the riot little bands of sullen, evil-looking men talked excitedly on street corners all over downtown Atlanta. Around seven o'clock my father and I were driving toward a mail box at the corner of Peachtree and Houston Streets when there came from near-by Pryor Street a roar the like of which I had never heard before, but which sent a sensation of mingled fear and excitement coursing through my body. I asked permission of Father to go and see what the trouble was. He bluntly ordered me to stay in the cart. A little later we drove down Atlanta's main business thoroughfare, Peachtree Street. Again we heard the terrifying cries, this time near at hand and coming toward us. We saw a lame Negro bootblack from Herndon's barber shop pathetically trying to outrun a mob of whites. Less than a hundred yards from us the chase ended. We saw clubs and fists descending to the accompaniment of savage shouting and cursing. Suddenly a voice cried, "There goes another nigger!" Its work done, the mob went after new prey. The body with the withered foot lay dead in a pool of blood on the street.

Father's apprehension and mine steadily increased during the evening, although the fact that our skins were white kept us from attack. Another circumstance favored us—the mob had not yet grown violent enough to attack

United States government property. But I could see Father's relief when he punched the time clock at eleven p.m. and got into the cart to go home. He wanted to go the back way down Forsyth Street, but I begged him, in my childish excitement and ignorance, to drive down Marietta to Five Points, the heart of Atlanta's business district, where the crowds were densest and the yells loudest. No sooner had we turned into Marietta Street, however, than we saw careening toward us an undertaker's barouche. Crouched in the rear of the vehicle were three Negroes clinging to the sides of the carriage as it lunged and swerved. On the driver's seat crouched a white man, the reins held taut in his left hand. A huge whip was gripped in his right. Alternately he lashed the horses and, without looking backward, swung the whip in savage swoops in the faces of members of the mob as they lunged at the carriage determined to seize the three Negroes.

There was no time for us to get out of its path, so sudden and swift was the appearance of the vehicle. The hub cap of the right rear wheel of the barouche hit the right side of our much lighter wagon. Father and I instinctively threw our weight and kept the cart from turning completely over. Our mare was a Texas mustang which, frightened by the sudden blow, lunged in the air as Father clung to the reins. Good fortune was with us. The cart settled back on its four wheels as Father said in a voice which brooked no dissent, "We are going home the back way and not down Marietta."

But again on Pryor Street we heard the cry of the mob. Close to us and in our direction ran a stout and elderly woman who cooked at a downtown white hotel. Fifty yards behind, a mob which filled the street from curb to curb was closing in. Father handed the reins to me and, though he was of slight stature, reached down and lifted the woman into the cart. I did not need to be told to lash the mare to the fastest speed she could muster.

The church bells tolled the next morning for Sunday service. But no one in Atlanta believed for a moment that the hatred and lust for blood had been appeased. Like skulls on a cannibal's hut the hats and caps of victims of the mob of the night before had been hung on the iron hooks of telegraph poles. None could tell whether each hat represented a dead Negro. But we knew that some of those who had worn the hats would never again wear any.

Late in the afternoon friends of my father's came to warn of more trouble that night. They told us that plans had been perfected for a mob to form on Peachtree Street just after nightfall to march down Houston Street to what the white people called "Darktown," three blocks or so below our house, to "clean out the niggers." There had never been a firearm in our house before that day. Father was reluctant even in those circumstances to violate the law, but he at last gave in at Mother's insistence.

We turned out the lights early, as did all our neighbors.

No one removed his clothes or thought of sleep. Apprehension was tangible. We could almost touch its cold and clammy surface. Toward midnight the unnatural quiet was broken by a roar that grew steadily in volume. Even today I grow tense in remembering it.

Father told Mother to take my sisters, the youngest of them only six, to the rear of the house, which offered more protection from stones and bullets. My brother George was away, so Father and I, the only males in the house, took our places at the front windows of the parlor. The windows opened on a porch along the front side of the house, which in turn gave onto a narrow lawn that sloped down to the street and a picket fence. There was a crash as Negroes smashed the street lamp at the corner of Houston and Piedmont Avenue down the street. In a very few minutes the vanguard of the mob, some of them bearing torches, appeared. A voice which we recognized as that of the son of the grocer with whom we had traded for many years yelled, "That's where that nigger mail carrier lives! Let's burn it down! It's too nice for a nigger to live in!" In the eerie light Father turned his drawn face toward me. In a voice as quiet as though he were asking me to pass him the sugar at the breakfast table, he said, "Son, don't shoot until the first man puts his foot on the lawn and then—don't you miss!"

In the flickering light the mob swayed, paused, and began to flow toward us. In that instant there opened up within me a great awareness; I knew then who I was. I was a Negro, a human being with an invisible pigmentation which marked me a person to be hunted, hanged, abused, discriminated against, kept in poverty and ignorance, in order that those whose skin was white would have readily at hand a proof of their superiority, a proof patent and inclusive, accessible to the moron and the idiot as well as to the wise man and the genius. No matter how low a white man fell, he could always hold fast to the smug conviction that he was superior to two-thirds of the world's population, for those two-thirds were not white.

It made no difference how intelligent or talented my millions of brothers and I were, or how virtuously we lived. A curse like that of Judas was upon us, a mark of degradation fashioned with heavenly authority. There were white men who said Negroes had no souls, and who proved it by the Bible. Some of these now were approaching us, intent upon burning our house.

Theirs was a world of contrasts in values: superior and inferior, profit and loss, cooperative and noncooperative, civilized and aboriginal, white and black. If you were on the wrong end of the comparison, if you were inferior, if you were noncooperative, if you were aboriginal, if you were black, then you were marked for excision, expulsion, or extinction. I was a Negro; I was therefore that part of history which opposed the good, the just, and the enlightened. I was a Persian, falling before the hordes of Alexander. I was a Carthaginian, extinguished by the Legions of Rome. I was a Frenchman at Waterloo, an Anglo-Saxon at Hastings, a Confederate at Vicksburg. I was the defeated, wherever and whenever there was a defeat.

Yet as a boy there in the darkness amid the tightening fright, I knew the inexplicable thing—that my skin was as white as the skin of those who were coming at me.

The mob moved toward the lawn. I tried to aim my gun, wondering what it would feel like to kill a man. Suddenly there was a volley of shots. The mob hesitated, stopped. Some friends of my father's had barricaded themselves in a two-story brick building just below our house. It was they who had fired. Some of the mobsmen, still bloodthirsty, shouted, "Let's go get the nigger." Others, afraid now for their safety, held back. Our friends, noting the hesitation, fired another volley. The mob broke and retreated up Houston Street.

In the quiet that followed I put my gun aside and tried to relax. But a tension different from anything I had ever known possessed me. I was gripped by the knowledge of my identity, and in the depths of my soul I was vaguely aware that I was glad of it. I was sick with loathing for the hatred which had flared before me that night and come so close to making me a killer; but I was glad I was not one of those who hated; I was glad I was not one of those made sick and murderous by pride. I was glad I was not one of those whose story is in the history of the world, a record of bloodshed, rapine, and pillage. I was glad my mind and spirit were part of the races that had not fully awakened, and who therefore had still before them the opportunity to write a record of virtue as a memorandum to Armageddon.

It was all just a feeling then, inarticulate and melancholy, yet reassuring in the way that death and sleep are reassuring, and I have clung to it now for nearly half a century.

from

THE GOOD TIMES
ARE KILLING ME

LYNDA BARRY

While apocalyptic moments of fire and death are the
most dramatic examples of coming of age, the movements of life are usually quite small and gradual, as
bits of knowledge and experience slowly weigh down
the pan. In this selection, cartoonist and novelist
Lynda Barry shows a young girl learning
more than she bargained for with the arrival
of a new record player.

My father came home one day with a present that I thought was going to change my life. It was my own record player that I had to share with Lucy. It was a little boxy thing, the kind that will only play 45s. He said he got it from a guy at work, but later I found out that it had belonged to the kids of a girl-friend we didn't know about yet. The one he would eventually marry and introduce to us one day by rolling down his car window and pointing his cigarette at a woman with a scarf on sitting across the seat from him, saying "That's your, your. . . , whaddaya call it. Your stepmother."

Before he gave the record player to us, he had the idea to spray it with a heavy coat of red enamel paint and he painted every part, including the needle and the masking tape holding the tone arm together. And he must have tried to pick it up when it was still wet because one day, a long time after he was gone, I found it sitting in the basement and I noticed for the first time the print of part of his hand on the side. It made me think of fossils, a million years old.

If you try to talk about my father to Lucy now, she'll say she doesn't remember nothing about him, but I think she is just being stubborn. I remember everything. Sometimes I remember so much I about hate him for it. Everybody was sad when he left. I think even the dogs in the street were sad.

When he had the days off sometimes we would play a game with him called "Get Lost," where he would take us on long rides all over in any direction and bet us our allowance that we couldn't get him lost. He would turn wherever we said, and when we'd ask him "Are you lost yet?" he'd say "Nope."

I have a song that automatically reminds me of him and sometimes when I hear it by accident I imagine that it secretly means he is thinking of me right then and the song is the sign of it. Sometimes it comes on the radio while we are eating dinner and I feel like I am seeing something in the room that no one else can see. Do you think it's possible that a song could be a message from someone?

And I don't know why that song would remind me of him because we never had the record of it and I never heard him singing it. It wasn't a special song to me at all. It was just a song that probably played on the radio all of the time when things were normal and I never even noticed that they were.

My mother has the same kind of song about him. It's called "Chances Are." Lucy put it on our red record player one day while my mother was in the basement with us folding laundry, and Mom started to sing with it and then all of a sudden she stopped. She put the clothes down, walked up the stairs, went inside her bedroom and closed the door.

• • •

In honor of our new record player, Lucy and I created the Record Player Night Club in the dark part of the basement between the door to the garage and the furnace with octopus arms twisting up in every direction. I knew right then that the record player was something very important to us, because normally both my sister and I avoided that furnace whenever possible.

We dragged over an old wooden table across the concrete floor and pulled out a long black extension cord that plugged in by the washer. We hammered nails in all over the walls and along the edges of the wooden table and hung the 152 records our dad gave us on each one. Then we both carried the record player down the stairs one step at a time slowly and carefully like it was a lighted birthday cake.

We picked out a record and put it on. It played. My sister and I just stood there trying to see the title of it while it went around and around. We could not believe how lucky we were.

We acted like we were inspectors from England and walked in and out of the room over and over again, pretending we had never seen anything like it before in our lives. We would point to the records hanging on the nails and go "I say my jolly old chap." We wanted to know exactly what a person would think who was seeing the room for the first time, and we decided they would think it looked incredible.

When Lucy held up a record made of clear red vinyl and looked through it, she said it made the room look even more incredible. Lucy told me it looked so good to her that she wished her eyes would just automatically see everything that way for the rest of her life. She ended up walking around the house looking through it so much that Mom had to take it away from her. Mom said it would ruin her eyes and besides, how was she supposed to concentrate anymore with Lucy always watching her through that red record?

The night we made the Record Player Night Club I couldn't sleep from thinking about more and more ideas for it. We could have parties. We could open up the door to the garage and have American Bandstand. We could set up charts for rating the records. "Is this record a Dream? Or a Dud?" We could spray paint every part of the whole room pure gold and people would come in and faint from the amazement of it. And finally I couldn't help it, I got out of bed and walked on my toes down the hall, and opened the basement door.

The concrete was freezing cold on my feet and I stood in the dark a long time waving my hand around before I found the string to pull on the light. The room was still exactly perfect. I started picking up records and pretending I was being interviewed on television about the room; how did I think up the idea for it, was I in fact a genius, was it hard to drag the table over, how many records did I have, all that.

I wanted to play a record so bad. I wondered for a long time if I played it really soft could they even hear it upstairs. And then I remembered I couldn't remember which way the loudness knob went and what if it was turned up the wrong way? I picked up the red record and looked at every wall through it and then I had the perfect idea.

In the darkroom our dad had set up under the basement steps there was a red light bulb. I took it and screwed it into a light in the Record Player Night Club. "Boy," I thought, "is Lucy ever going to be surprised." Being in the pitch dark Record Player Night Club when only the red light was on would put us in a perfect mood to listen to records because music sounds so completely different in the dark.

In our night club we invented this dance where we would put the lighted end of a flashlight in our mouths and just move around in slow motion with our cheeks lit up like we were just sad, lonely ghosts who loved all music except for one certain song that would suddenly make us go wild and strangle people, and we were doing this dance when Bonna Willis first pounded on the door that led in from the garage to the record room. You better believe it made us jump.

There are good things about Bonna Willis and there are

bad things about Bonna Willis, and right now I shouldn't be caring about any of them because right now we hate each other's guts and I don't guess that is going to change this June the way it usually does when school is out. Now that we're older you can bet all of that's over. I already know she won't be caught dead talking to no little honky girl this year, and the same goes for her from me only backwards using the word I won't say.

The only reason me and Bonna ever ended up friends in the first place is because when it would finally get hot outside, and everybody in our neighborhood would take their inner tubes and go down to the lake, we were the only ones left stuck on this stupid street. I could never go to the lake because I might drown and Bonna could never go because her little brother did drown. Yeah he drownt. He drownt and that is part of the reason Bonna's mother acts the way she does and another part of the reason Bonna can't ever go no more than two blocks from her house except for school, to keep an eye on her in case her mother tries to do something funny again like go down Crowley hill in just a robe and shower cap, but even I can't stand to remember that because I like Bonna's mother. I knew her from when before Elvin died and she was still acting OK. Elvin wasn't the only one of them who died you know, because there was another brother named Cleveland who got shot by accident in Washington D.C. where Bonna lived before they had to come out here to just get away from trouble.

They've got a school picture of him up on their wall and I have stared at it many times even though I feel embarrassed at how he's just smiling and not knowing nothing about what is going to happen to him. I know. Me, a girl he never met in a town he never even saw knows exactly the ending and even after the ending. How his whole family moves away afterwards and leaves the place where he used to live, leaves all the sidewalks and the steps and the doors he used to open and shut, and comes all the way out here to my street. I know how his sister is going to hate this place so much that one time she shouts that she hates him too for making them come here, and how her father will cross that living room flying and slap her across the face in front of He Don't Give A Damn Who. And how that picture of Cleveland smiling will just hang there and hang there on the wall in a house on a street in a city he could never have dreamed of even if he dreamed a hundred million dreams.

Sometimes I start thinking what happened to all his things? His pencils, his shirt, his comb, his shoes, his everything, until I just have to close my eyes and think of something else.

And other times I want to memorize that picture. Know every part of it. You'd think you could run out of things to notice in one picture pretty fast, but you don't. Every time I look at it I can find something new. Like his chipped tooth or the way the one side of his collar is turned under. How he wrote his name in the corner slanted up and underlined. The way you can tell the pen wouldn't work right, how he had to go over each letter until you could read it: Love From Your Loving Son.

The last time I was there—and I couldn't believe I never noticed it before—I saw a tiny chickenpox scar on his cheek in the exact same place Lucy has one.

I remember once in a magazine I saw three pictures of a man who died falling out of a hot air balloon. They showed him getting closer and closer to the ground. One. Two. Three.

Doesn't it seem that if you can take a picture of the thing before it happens, you can stop it? You can stop time long enough to at least yell a warning?

I imagine being able to go back into that picture of Cleveland and save him. I imagine being able to go back and whisper "Look out" into his ear.

And after I saved him, well, maybe he would beg me to be his girlfriend.

Back then, the day she first pounded on the door of the Record Player Night Club, all I knew about Bonna was that I had to watch out for her, everybody did. Because she would get after you for no reason, swearing to beat the asses of everyone in our neighborhood on a rotating basis. That was the main topic of her conversation: ass beating. And it wasn't just all talk and no action either. I guess she's just about the best ass beater I have ever met in my life, boys included.

The news got out to her about us having our own record player and when I opened the door Lucy took the flashlight out of her mouth and shined it right into Bonna's face and said "You have the right to remain silent," and I about fell over when I saw it was her standing there with about ten records she wanted to play. That was a long time ago because Elvin was still alive then and she had him with her, and we still had the rule of no Negro kids can come in our house. At first I worried about how was I supposed to explain the rule to Bonna, and then I suddenly realized that we were in the basement and the door came into it from the garage. It would be OK because they could come inside without ever coming inside the real part of the house.

I had never really seen Bonna close up and the first thing I noticed about her was that for earrings she had little pieces of broom straws with the ends burnt, stuck through her ears.

I asked her way later what was the first thing she noticed about me and she said how much I looked like the what-me-worry guy on the Mad magazine, but she wasn't saying it for offense. You can't control the first thing you notice about someone.

Bonna's records had a screaming sound that I had never heard before, but I tried to look like naturally I had heard them all about a million times. There would be a man screaming;

and I really mean screaming, and then all of these people would scream back. She said the man's name was James Brown and told me that the song he was singing was called "Say It Loud, I'm Black and I'm Proud." I had never heard of being proud about being a Negro so I wondered was this a joke song or what? She told me that black panthers were coming to beat the whitey's ass and I didn't know what she was talking about, so I said "I know that. Who doesn't know that?"

She put on another record and told me she was going to do a dance that her cousin showed her called the Tighten Up. "I know that dance," I said.

"Prove it," she said.

I stood there looking at her. "I don't feel like it," I said.

"You lie you die," she said and that made Lucy laugh and say "you lie you die" over and over like it was the best poem she ever heard in her life.

"I'll show you how," Bonna said. "I just learned it from my cousin so I know no one out here knows it yet." She put the needle on the record. "Stand over here," she said, pointing next to her. "Go sideways like this and move your one hand around fast like this and move the other one over like this and when they say the part 'Now make it mellow,' move your arms like this." And she bit on her lips and moved her hands in the shape of tornados.

"I said I just don't feel like it, OK?" and I hoped she would just forget about it.

Bonna said "Watch Elvin do it, come here Elvin, do the Tighten Up, watch him watch him, yeah Elvin come ON! Come ON! He funny, ain't he? Elvin, you think you sly? Look at how he thinks he sly!"

Elvin was only five. I watched him do the mellow part thing perfectly and I felt so completely cheated out of something and I can't even tell you what. Lucy did it too, but she was only Elvin's age so it didn't matter yet how stupid she looked.

Later, after they left and we went upstairs, I told Lucy we had better not tell Mom about Bonna and Elvin, and Lucy nodded her head.

That night I imagined me and Bonna becoming best friends. What that would be like and how everyone in the neighborhood would start to be afraid of me the same way they were afraid of her. I imagined naming the Record Player Night Club "Edna and Bonna's Record Player Night Club at Edna's," and her being so honored by it she would beat the ass of anyone I said. And I saw myself being able to do the Tighten Up so perfectly that people would faint from it. Me and Bonna in the front of the lunchroom during assembly, doing the Tighten Up for the President's Council on Fitness. "First Place Award. Now announcing the winners—Edna Arkins and Bonna Willis." We would put the trophy in our Night Club.

I lay there under the covers thinking all about it, watching headlights slide across the wall and listening to Lucy breathing.

For a little while, after Mom got sick and all she could do was stay in her bed with the curtains shut and the lights off, begging God out loud to please make us be quiet, it was Bonna's mother Mrs. Willis who took us to church. But we didn't go to our regular church. We went to a different church that was inside an old store on a street where when we drove down it, our mom would always say "Are your doors locked? Lock your doors so the bogey-man won't get you." It was in the part of town where Mom would point out every police car she saw and tell us to wave.

My sister leaned over to me and whispered "What kind of church is this anyway?" but I tried to sit as normal as possible on a folding chair more beat up than the ones at school, and look like I had been there one thousand times. We sat with Bonna's mother and Elvin, but Bonna sat in the front with some other girls from my school and they were all wearing long gorgeous red robes. A man got up and started to talk and talk and talk, then comes a lady in a beautiful blue tent dress with patterns of golden swirled in it and she had giant arms and her name was Sister I can't remember what. And she sits down at the piano watching the man talk and talk and when he looks at her and smiles she starts to play and begins to sing a song like I had never heard in my life. I couldn't believe perfect singing like that could come out of a real person, a real person who I could go over to and touch with my finger.

She sang with her eyes closed tight, but she was moving her head around like she was watching something and suddenly she made her voice go so low it wasn't even like a lady's anymore and that is when Bonna's mother made me jump by shouting "Go ON! YES!" The more she sang the more people shouted, telling her to go, go, go like it was a race they wanted her to win, and she played faster, and when I looked away from her I saw Bonna in her red robe standing at the front of the room with the other kids, swaying on one foot two times and then the other foot two times and Bonna looked across the room at me and when they started to sing, everyone in the church stood up and started to sing and I looked all around for the hymn book. Where were they getting the song? Where were they getting the words? People were clapping and jumping and I could feel the floor bouncing and the man takes the microphone and shouts into it "YES! COME ON CHURCH! YES! GOD IS MOVING CAN YOU FEEL HIM MOVING!" and I look around and the whole place has gone crazy talking to themselves, pounding their feet, crying, reaching their hands in the air for I don't know what, saying yes lord yes lord and thank you jesus yes my jesus. And that lady is playing the piano so hard I feel the world start to spin, and then Lucy reaches over and starts to yank on my clothes the way she does to Mom when she is scared, and I reach over and pull her arm to stand her up and try to get her to act like everybody else so we won't stand out so bad.

I wondered would we get in trouble for this? It was an accident. We didn't know. We thought this was going to be a regular church. You act like this in our church and the priest will send you straight to hell.

After it was over, Lucy and I walked out onto the sidewalk squinting our eyes from the light and stood beside the Willises' car. We saw everybody in front of the church shaking hands, laughing, touching each other on the back and giving kisses, with all the kids running in circles around them, everybody acting like what they all just did in there was the most ordinary thing in the world.

The summer I met Bonna none of the teenagers on our block could drive yet and they would all come out onto the street after dinner shouting and chasing each other, doing what my dad called grab-assing, and the rest of us would play three-hour kick ball games in the intersection until it was too dark to see.

And some nights the older boys did a kind of dance

parade where they would all get into a line and start singing these things, these poems, about a girl I didn't know named Tracy Sloan, and Bonna told me they were cold blooded poems. The author was Earl Stelly, who would whistle through his fingers and start walking in a way called the Pimp Walk. That was the summer we all wanted to be pimps when we grew up. We didn't really know a lot about pimps except they wore great clothes and jewelry, had nice cars and walked cool, and all of the other boys would jump in line behind Earl Stelly, clapping their hands and slapping their legs and chests, leaning far over stroking their chins and walking the Pimp Walk, chanting "UH! Ahhhh. I Said UH! Ahhh," until they would sound like a train going up and down the block with Earl in front pointing his finger around and singing out his famous poem, "Is Tracy Sloan Like a Cake?" with the boys shouting out the answers. And Earl Stelly must have really loved her, too, because he even had the color of her shoes in that poem. I always wanted to see her, see what was the big deal about Tracy Sloan, but she lived way up on the Crest, on Circle View, somewhere you would never leave to come down over to the street where we lived.

We all thought Earl Stelly was great because he could make up poems about anything. He would do this imitation of a preacher where he would climb up on a car and say "The name is Preacher Deacon Reverend Stelly and I am here to send your asses to fry up in hell." He'd call us Brother and

Sister and would sing these preaches, poems about the Bible like "David Messed Up Goliath's Head" that he told us he invented, but Bonna told me he was lying because she heard the same poems before on a record. He'd sing the lines one by one, making a noise deep in his throat like he could hardly breathe. One of his poems went:

> *Brother Abel was a nigger boy*
> *Brother Cain he was a whitey*
> *Got out into the field one day*
> *Got in a little fighty.*
> *Brother Cain kill Abel with a rock*
> *Then Abel jumped up from the dead*
> *Took out his Colt revolver*
> *Shot Cain all full of lead.*

He was shouting and rocking the car with his legs until he turned and saw his mother standing on the porch holding a dish rag and watching him and listening to him and did you know it turns out Earl's father was a real preacher?

When Mrs. Stelly was done yelling at him, she turned around and went inside and every one of us just stood there until Earl jumped off that car and tore off down Crowley, and if I were him I would have just kept right on going until I reached the other end of the world.

• • •

For a while after school, before I was old enough to take care of Lucy by myself, we'd have to walk all the way up to Aunt Margaret's and stay there until my mom got home from work. Both Lucy and I hated that because Aunt Margaret wanted us to stay in the basement all of the time to keep us from messing up the plastic she had on her new furniture, and there wasn't anything to do there except sit around on their old couch in the part she called their future rec room and read or cut pictures out of old magazines while listening to my cousin Steve practice the trumpet. After we complained about it so much, Mom finally fixed it with my aunt to have my cousin Ellen come over and baby sit us for twenty-five cents for the two hours until Mom got home, which Ellen said was a gyp because Aunt Margaret just took the money from her to put toward her college education.

This was a long time ago when Ellen was in junior high school and still stuck up and mean. A lot of times her best friend Sharon would come with her and they would sit in our kitchen acting big and smoking the cigarettes they stole from Sharon's mom, who must have had a pile of them not to notice. Ellen hated us and I knew it but I loved her and Sharon because they were both so beautiful and developed. I didn't even care when they invented a game of ignoring Lucy and me, saying "Did you hear something? It must have been the wind," whenever we would try to talk to them. In a way it was good because if I didn't exist, they couldn't tell me to go bug off when I sat there on the floor leaning against the stove watching them and listening to every word they said and imagining how great it would be to be them.

When we made the Record Player Night Club all I could think about was wait until Ellen saw it. She would realize I was a genius and she'd start begging me to spend the night with her and go downtown with her and always hang around with her for the rest of her life, amen. I practiced how at first I would say "Nope. No way. Serves you right for ignoring me so much all those times," and then after she begged and begged and begged I'd finally give in and she would be so happy we would wear matching clothes and she would put makeup on me like she did one time before she became such a snob.

I sat on the back steps with Lucy waiting for them to come around the corner and it seems like it took a million years, and when I finally saw them I stood up to unlock the back door with Lucy pushing behind me.

"I get to show them," Lucy says.

"No way Lucy," I say. "I'm showing them." It wouldn't do Lucy any good to show them. She was way too young to hang around with Ellen and me anyway.

"Then I'm coming with. I am," Lucy said. Why did she always have to be so stupid about everything?

"Aren't either, so forget it," I said, and I pushed her and she fell off the steps. I said I was sorry and I tried to tell her I didn't mean to push her that hard but she started crying anyway. Lucy went into our bedroom and slammed the door and I heard Sharon say to Ellen, "What's wrong with the little brat?" and if I wasn't so in love with her I would have kicked her in the leg for calling Lucy that.

It took me a long time to make Ellen and Sharon act like they could hear me and come down into the basement. But when they came down the stairs behind me all I could think of was how they were not going to be able to believe how mod it was.

I told them to stand by the washer and just wait a second.

I pulled on the string and the light came on red. I turned a song on the record player. Then I stood in the middle of the room and yelled "OK!" and watched them walk in.

"Neat!" said Ellen.

"Wicked!" said Sharon.

Ellen picked one of my favorite 45s off of the nail and read Sharon the title. "'Birddog.' By The Everly Brothers. God, I just love that song, don't you, Shar?" and then I saw her turn her head to hide that she was laughing. Sharon picked up a record and said "Ellen, 'Volare!' Your favorite!" And she handed Ellen the record and Ellen said to me "Come on Ed, let me borrow this one. I just have to borrow this, OK? Please?" and then they both started laughing.

That was the day I finally learned that it's not good enough just to have a record player and a bunch of records. You have to have a bunch of the right records. And it doesn't matter if you like the records you have because there are only certain songs that are good to listen to. All the rest are corny. It turned out all the ones that we had were corny.

Ellen asked me if I was going to have a Shindig party here sometime and would I invite her, and I told her to just go shut up and flake off and get out and drop dead and they acted like I had just told them the funniest joke in the world.

DON: THE TRUE STORY OF A YOUNG PERSON

GARRISON KEILLOR

The revolutionary importance of rock and roll has nothing to do with swinging hips and suggestive lyrics. Its real value is that it has let the youth of the last fifty years express the unique concerns and confusions presented by growing up. In this comic story by Garrison Keillor, a midwestern garage band finds the coming complications of adulthood in the controversy regarding one poorly considered moment of their stage show.

Earl and Mavis Beeman and son Don, seventeen, had lived together in the two-bedroom green-stucco house at 2813 Rochester for sixteen years, but for the last two they had been like ships in the night. Don, a gangly youth with his father's large head and flat nose and his mother's shoulder-length hair, kept to himself and seldom spoke unless spoken to. "Ever since he joined that band . . ." his dad said. Mavis suspected drugs and finally asked Don straight out. He told her that coffee is a drug, but, as Mavis pointed out, coffee drinkers do not lock themselves in their rooms and never talk to their parents.

Actually, Don did love his folks. It was just that right now he was totally into his music. But they thought something was wrong. One Friday night, when Don and his band, Trash, were playing for a dance at the Armory, Earl and Mavis went in and shook down his room. Under the bed they found a box of tapes, numbered 1 through 4 and marked Songs. They played them and found out they were songs written and sung by Don. They were about subjects he had never discussed at home, such as anger and violence. One song was about going down the street and tripping up nuns, and although the Beemans were not Catholic, they were shocked.

The next morning, Earl spoke to Don. He didn't mention the songs, but he told Don to quit being moody around home and to make good use of his time, instead of hanging around with a bunch of punks who were up to no good. "We didn't bring you up to be just another dumb punk," Earl told him. "Sometimes you make me ashamed to be your parent."

Actually, punk rock, as it is called, has brought about some useful changes in popular music, as many respected rock critics have pointed out, and its roots can be traced back to the very origins of rock itself and perhaps even a little bit farther. "It goes without saying," Green Phillips has written in *Rip It Up: The Sound of the American Urban Experiment*, "that punk rock is outrageous. Outrage is its object, its *raison d'être,* its very soul. It can also be said to be mean, filthy, stupid, self-destructive, and a menace to society. But that does not mean we should minimize its contribution or fail to see it for what it truly is: an attempt to reject the empty posturing of the pseudo-intellectual album-oriented Rock-as-Art consciousness cult of the post-*Pepper* era and to recreate the primal persona of the Rocker as Car Thief, Dropout, and Guy Who Beats Up Creeps."

Punk-rock bands, Phillips goes on to say, through their very outrageousness—the musicians spitting onstage, cursing and throwing things at the audience, breaking up dressing rooms, trying to burn down auditoriums, and sometimes seriously injuring their managers and road crews—have forced many critics to re-examine certain pre-punk assumptions, such as the role of criticism.

As it turned out, criticism was exactly what Earl gave Don, especially after the President's Day County 4-H Poultry Show dance, at which Trash played. Actually, the dance wasn't so bad. The band was rowdy and yelled a lot of tough, punk types of stuff at the audience, but that was their thing, after all, and nobody really minded until Trash's drummer, Bobby Thompson, spat at Sharon Farley while she was being crowned Poultry Show Queen on the stage between numbers. He said that she had given him a stuck-up look, but Mrs. Goodrich, the senior 4-H Club adviser, ordered him to leave the poultry barn instantly. But the kids thought it had been done just in fun, and yelled until she decided to let him stay, on condition that he didn't do any more of that sort of thing.

Of course, this was a direct challenge to the others in the band. Brian Bigelow, the bass player, spat at Mrs. Goodrich as she left the stage, and then, with the crowd yelling and egging them on, the others in the band made belching noises and lifted up their shirts. Don and the other guitarist, Art Johnson, turned their amps up full blast, and soon feed pellets were flying back and forth. Things were just about completely out of hand when suddenly a guy tossed a chicken on the stage and Bobby grabbed it and bit its neck.

Instantly, the barn was hushed. "Did you *see* that!" some people murmured. "See *what?*" other people whispered. Trash packed up their equipment quickly, while several exhibitors chased and then caught the chicken. Somebody took it to a vet. Everyone went home.

The next morning at breakfast, Earl picked up the *Gazette* and found his son on page 1. "4-H DANCE ENDS IN RIOT AS ROCK BAND EATS LIVE BIRD," the headline said. According to the story, police were investigating the incident, which one observer at the scene called "an act of bestiality reminiscent of Nazi Germany."

Earl, a veteran of the Second World War, exploded. He kicked open Don's bedroom door, flung himself at his son, who had only just awakened, and hauled him out of bed by one leg. "Why?" he screamed. "Why? Why? Why?" He swung wildly at the dumbfounded youth with the rolled-up newspaper.

"Why do you do everything possible to disgrace us?" he yelled. "Why must you search for ways to show your hatred and contempt? Even if you have no respect for us, do you have no respect for yourself? How can you do this? Is there no limit?"

"Dad," Don said when Earl finally paused for breath. "Dad, it's only music."

"It's only music," Earl repeated dumbly. "It's only music. You drag our name in the mud, and you say it's only music. I suppose the next thing you'll tell me is it's only a chicken!"

Actually, it *was* only a chicken, as Don and his friends kept telling each other when they met that night in Bobby's garage to rehearse. They hadn't shot a deer or gutted a fish or slaughtered a pig or thrown a lobster into a pot of boiling water. One of them, in the excitement of the moment, had simply bitten the neck of a chicken—a chicken that, as it turned out, was going to be perfectly O.K. They had the vet's word on that.

"They are trying to pin on us all the violence and hatred that are in their own hearts," said Brian, hanging up his big bass speaker on a rafter. "They think our music is violent just because it shows them where *they* are at and they don't dare to admit it."

"They can try all they want but they'll never stop rock and roll," Bobby said, referring to Mrs. Goodrich, who had already called up all of the county 4-H Club advisers, several youth ministers, a lot of high school teachers, and the county extension agent to arrange an emergency meeting that night.

"TEEN LEADERS VOW ANTI-ROCK DRIVE, AIM SMUT BAN IN AREA," the *Gazette* reported the following morning. "Long-time youth worker Diane Goodrich enjoys having a good time as much as the next person [the story went on], but Monday night, watching a local rock band rip into a live chicken with their teeth at the 4-H Poultry Show dance, she decided it was time to call 'foul.' Evidently, more than a few people agree with her. Last night, at a meeting in the high school auditorium attended on a word-of-mouth basis by literally dozens of parents, not to mention civic leaders and youth advisers, she spoke for the conscience of a community when she said, 'Have we become so tolerant of deviant behavior, so sympathetic toward the sick in our society, that, in the words of Bertram Follette, we have lost the capacity to say, This is not far out. You have simply gone too far. Now we say No!?'"

Don walked slowly home from school that day. A B+ student, he was sensitive to the accusations made against him and his friends, and while he knew that the uproar had been caused at least partly by irresponsible reporting in the media, he also realized that the time had come for both sides to cool their rhetoric and sit down and talk. In his mind, he sought ways for his dad and himself to resolve their differences, but he couldn't think of a single one. Actually, their relationship had been pretty good—at least, on a hunting-and-fishing level. Earl had taught Don how to handle a shotgun and tie a fly and clean a fish and take care of a skillet and, most of all, how to sit still all morning in the blind. Actually, that was a problem. In hunting and fishing, it is important, of course, to be absolutely quiet. Don and Earl had spent whole days on Stone Lake casting into rocky inlets for bass, and if Don so much as rattled an oarlock Earl glared at him. Don was never encouraged to share with his dad his feelings about himself or his hopes for the future. He was expected to sit and not scare fish.

• • •

It was a shaken Trash, an incensed Trash, that met in the Thompsons' garage after supper on Wednesday. "We're going to show them," Brian vowed, his fists clenched white, "that we can be everything they say we are. They tell lies about us—O.K., we're going to make those lies come true!"

That night, they played with wild abandon. The garage windows rattled as the band members blew off their frustration at having been attacked for something that had been blown up way out of proportion.

> Baby, you call me an animal for something I didn't do,
> Well, if that's how you want it I'm going to be wild for you!

At the word "wild," the boys lunged forward and crouched and grinned like madmen.

> Well, O.K., baby, you think you're Little Red Riding Hood,
> I'll be the Big Bad Wolf, and this time I'll get you good.

Here, Art stomped on the blitz pedal, throwing his amp into overdrive, while Don beat on his Ripley B-19 with windmill chops, and Brian actually straddled the bass and rode it like a horse. Bobby leaped from the drums and, with one yank, started up his father's lawn mower, to which they had taped a microphone.

> I'm gonna ride my mower all around this town
> Cut everybody who's been trying to put me down!

Now they moved into the finale. The lawn mower was stopped and the band fell silent; except for the *bump-bump-bump* of Brian's bass, as Bobby staggered forward like somebody completely out of his mind—panting, groping, and stumbling, with his eyes wild—while Brian sang:

> Well, you call us trash, so what do we have to lose?
> We're gonna be so bad you can read it in the morning news!

Suddenly Bobby leaped into the air, rushed forward, reached into a cardboard box, and grabbed a chicken and bit it again and again, until the feathers flew.

Actually, it was just a pillow they had put there for the rehearsal, but it seemed real to Trash, who sat back exhausted after the song. They all had experienced a tremendous release from it, and yet they were stunned at what had happened.

"Like I wasn't even aware of what I was doing," Bobby said. "I couldn't believe it was me. It was that great."

"It's bigger than us," Art said. "I get into it and I am just completely blown away."

"I don't know if we should actually ever do it," Don said. "If you think we really should, then I guess so, but I really don't know."

"I don't think we should do it unless we're really into it, but if it's going to happen, then I say let it happen," Brian said.

• • •

On Wednesday evening, Earl and Mavis were sitting in their forest-green lounger chairs beside the fireplace in the basement family room, reading the sports and family sections, respectively, of the *Gazette*. There was more about Mrs. Goodrich and her Committee for Teen Decency on the family page ("ROCK-RECORD ROAST SLATED FOR SUNDAY"), but by now Mavis was able to read articles on the subject without tears. "I don't know, I feel they are being unfair to Don and his friends," she said to Earl. "They are making a mountain out of what was probably just a joke. Mrs. Thompson told me that Bobby didn't even draw blood on that chicken. All it suffered was a slight neck sprain. She said that when Bobby was little he would tease his sister by pretending to eat angleworms. Maybe this is the same thing."

"Time they grew up, then," Earl said. "They walk around like they got the world on a string. Never listen to a thing you say. Treat you like dirt. Maybe this'll give them a taste of their own medicine."

"I don't know," Mavis said thoughtfully. "A mother doesn't have all the answers. Sometimes I'm upset by little things they do or say. Sometimes I wonder. But in the end I know he's still my boy. I may not always understand, but I know he needs me to be here, to listen, to forgive. And I know there's nobody so bad but what they deserve a second chance."

Earl and Mavis talked a long time that night. They remembered the many good times they had had with

Don—the pleasure he had given them, the many wonderful memories. Mavis recalled that Don's first word had been Papa, and Earl recalled that his second was chicken. They both had a good laugh over that.

"They were good years, Mave," Earl said, his eyes glistening. "I've been wrong about Don. I'll do better now."

"Tomorrow is a new day," she replied brightly.

"He's a good boy if only we'd give him a chance," said Earl, practically weeping.

"Just like his daddy," said Mavis, reaching for his hand.

"Let's go to bed," said Earl, rising. He held her tightly.

"I think this is just going to bring us closer together," she said.

Don couldn't sleep Wednesday night. He had gotten up twice, once to swipe a pack of his dad's Salems and then to get the blackberry wine left over from Christmas, and now, as he lay in bed drinking and smoking and carefully exhaling toward the fan that hummed in the window, he felt torn between his deep love of music and his fears that Trash was going off the deep end. He had confessed this doubt to Brian at school, and Brian said, "If it feels good, then what's wrong?" Don was not completely certain in his own mind if this made sense or not. How can you feel good if you don't know it's right, he wondered. And how do you know if something is right?

After talking to Brian, he had spent his lunch hour in the library, searching the short shelf marked Philosophy & Religion for a book that might clarify his thinking, and now he reached for it on the bedside table. It was *The Art of Decision-Making,* by M. Henry Fellows. A paragraph from the preface had impressed him, and now he read it again:

> In a society appearing often paralyzed by an overload of complex decisions, the act of decision-making may assume primary importance over the actual meaning and effect of the decision itself; or, to put it another way, a crucial function of the decision-making process is to assert the power to decide. It is necessary to make this point absolutely clear: in an increasingly complicated society, the act of making decisions is clearly not a matter of choice but a matter of necessity.

Once again Don knew he must decide whether to stay in Trash and risk banishment from home and the permanent hatred of a community (and perhaps a nation) united in outrage at the senseless injury (or even death) of a barnyard fowl, or not, and he had to decide before their next public appearance.

The next morning, Mavis got on the phone to the other

Trash parents, and that evening, in the Beeman living room, the eight of them agreed that the boys had been treated unfairly and deserved a second chance. "Let's put on a dance ourselves!" Art's mom suggested, and everybody said, "Why not?" That week, Earl arranged through his union to rent the Bricklayers Hall for a low rate, and Mrs. Thompson, who worked for an ad agency, formed her media friends into a publicity committee. Mavis took charge of refreshments, and Mr. Thompson talked the mayor, an old fishing buddy, into granting them a provisional dance permit. "We'll have to move fast before the City Council can rescind it," he said. "Saturday night's the night."

Trash rehearsed Thursday night in the Thompson's garage. Although they knew their folks had gotten behind them, they didn't discuss the planned dance, now tentatively titled (Mrs. Thompson's idea) A Salute to Youth. Perhaps they couldn't believe it was true. Once again the music was so powerful, so all-encompassing, that the boys got carried away and went right into "They Call Us Trash." "Let's not do that song tonight," Don had asked, but they did—they couldn't help it—and they played even more wildly than before, perhaps because of a strobe light that Art had borrowed from his dad, a mechanic, who used it for balancing wheels. The effect of the strobe was frightening. Bobby ate practically half the pillow before they could get it away from him. They had to sit on him and hold him down, even though they were pretty shaky themselves. When they had quieted down a little, they tried out Brian's new song, which he had written that day:

> All my life you told me "Shut up and behave."
> Well, from now on, Mama, your boy's gonna scream and rave.
> I know you hate to see me playing rock and roll,
> But Mom, I gotta break your heart to save my soul.

Later on, Don would remember the last line as the point at which he had begun to make his decision.

Don came home from school Friday and, as usual, put on a record and fixed himself a peanut-butter-on-toast sandwich and a glass of milk. The phone rang just as the toast popped up. "Long distance calling for a Donald Beeman," said an operator's voice.

"This is him," Don answered.

"Go ahead," she said.

"Don," said a deep voice at the other end. "Green Phillips here, at *Falling Rocks.*"

Falling Rocks! At the mention of the name of the country's leading rock tabloid, Don's mind went completely numb. *Falling Rocks!* But—

"Don, we have a photographer who is flying out there right now on a chartered jet to cover your concert tomorrow," Phillips went on. "I'll be doing the story from here, and I need something from you over the phone. I'm going upstairs in a minute and I'm going to try to sell this thing as a cover story, but at the moment I'm up against a Beatles-reunion rumor and a Phil Spector retrospective and God knows what else, so I need something to put us over the top. Don, I'm going to put it straight to you. I'm up against a bunch of editors who don't know what's going on, and I need to know something right now—not tonight, not tomorrow morning, not maybe, but yes or no. Is your guy going to eat the chicken or isn't he?"

"What did you tell him?" Bobby grabbed Don's shoulders and shook him and hugged him at the same time.

"I said probably."

"Probably?"

"I said yes, I was pretty sure, it looked like that was going to happen."

"It's in the *bank!*" Bobby yelled. "It's not *going* to happen. It's *happening!*"

"Geek Rock is a style that departs radically from the punk genre even as it transcends it," Green Phillips explained in the cover story he typed out that night. "It is music with a mythic urge, raw and dirty and yet soaring off into the cosmic carny spirit of primitivist America and the sawdust world of the freak show of the soul, starring Tamar, Half Girl and Half Gorilla, and Koko, the Wild Man from Borneo Who Eats Live Spiders.

"For all the macho leather and scarred brilliance of its Presleys, Vincents, or Coopers," he wrote, "rock has always stayed within the bounds of urban sensibility—a more ordered world that has filed rebellion and outrage into the thematic grid of heavy drinking, hard fighting, hot cars, and fast sex. The achievement of Trash is to take us, as punk rock never can, into the darkest backroads of the heartland, back into the sideshow tent of the American experience, and, inevitably, of course, back into ourselves."

On Saturday morning, Don slept late, and when he awoke he longed to go downstairs and plead with his mom and dad, "Please cancel A Salute to Youth. Don't ask why—just cancel it immediately," he wanted to tell them. But he knew it was too late for reappraisal. Whatever was going to happen had gained too much momentum.

The three hundred friends and relatives of Trash who jammed the Bricklayers Hall that night (including a number of ministers who believed that the basic message of rock was caring and sharing, as well as Don's grandma, who was hard of hearing) knew no such trepidation. They piled into the hall as if they were going to a party. It took Mr. Thompson, who was master of ceremonies, several minutes to get all the people to take their seats and give him their attention. He spoke briefly on the importance of trust in human relationships and then, to brighten the occasion with a little humor, he shouted, "And now, back *safe and sound* from its last engagement . . ." and waved toward the wings, and out came the treasurer of the 4-H Club bearing a chicken with a bandaged neck. He put it down in its cage at the front of the stage, and the crowd gave the chicken a standing ovation.

Trash leaped out onstage, ready to play for keeps. "We Come to Rock," "Look Out, Danger," "Electric Curtains," "It Hurts Me More," and "Dirty, Desperate, Born to Die" (all originals) led off the show and were appreciated by almost everyone. Many people in the crowd, including all the Trash parents, got up to dance to the crackling beat, which seemed to pound through the floor. Some of the parents had learned this particular dance in adult-education classes. "They certainly do get quite a sound out of secondhand instruments!" Mrs. Thompson called to Mavis Beeman. Mavis was nervous. "Don't they look a little feverish to you?" she asked. Don had actually been feeling sick all day. His face was flushed and his stomach was upset, but he had refused to let his mother take his temperature. "Nothing at all," he said when she asked what was wrong. But later he came into the kitchen during supper and said maybe it would be better if she and Earl stayed home tonight, that it might be too late for them.

"Of course not," she had said. "We *want* to be there."

Now it was eleven o'clock—they had promised the Bricklayers to be through by eleven-thirty—and, standing at the back of the hall, trying to see over the dancers, Mavis was stricken by the sight of the chicken, still up there in its cage. She didn't know why, but she felt sure that if she could only reach the stage in time... "Stop the music!" she cried. She pushed forward into the waves and currents of bodies, which shoved and battered against her as the band sang, "You call me an animal for something I didn't do."

"Don, it's not too late!" she hollered, but it was, and her efforts only served to give her a front-row seat for a sight she would never forget the rest of her life: a brief moment of eye contact with a chicken as it fixed her with an expression of utter reproach in the split second before Bobby tore open the cage.

"Perhaps no bird, not even the eagle, bluebird, or robin, has entered so deeply the folk consciousness of the race as has the common chicken (*Gallus gallus*)," Green Phillips had written. "Indeed, throughout the Christian world, and even in many non-Christian countries, the chicken, from Plymouth Rock to lowly Leghorn, has come to stand for industry, patience, and fecundity, and, through its egg, for life itself, rebirth, and the resurrection of Christ, and, through its soup, for magical healing and restoration of the spirit. And yet, even as the chicken rides high as symbol of the Right Life in the pastoral dreams of the post-agrarian bourgeoisie, its name has attracted other connotations—of pettiness, timidity, and foolishness—perhaps reflecting our culture's doubts about itself. It is the peculiar genius of Trash to exploit this dichotomy to its fullest resolution, and thus to release in an audience such revulsion as can only indicate that profound depths have been reached."

• • •

Trash spent Saturday night at the Thompsons'. Mrs. Thompson had said that she would not speak to them but she would not turn them away, either, and they were welcome to sleep in the basement. Mr. Thompson was out consoling the Beemans, who had taken it hard, especially Mavis. Don called home Sunday afternoon, and his mom hung up on him.

Trash spent Sunday night on a bus to Omaha and put up at a Holiday Inn, and on Monday night played one set as an opening act to Sump, at the Armory. Advance ticket sales had been sluggish for weeks, until the promoter booked Trash on the strength of a page 2 photo in the Sunday paper showing Bobby with a faceful of feathers under the headline "CHICKEN SLAIN BY MIDWEST SINGER." Quickly reprinted on posters, it boosted box office some, but in the drafty hall, playing on borrowed gear to a strange and scattered audience, Trash couldn't work up to the emotional peak they needed to make the whole thing work. The new chicken sat in its cage and shivered, and when the time came Bobby hadn't the heart to do more that just pick it up and shake it. The crowd, which naturally expected more, booed them off the stage.

But actually it wasn't bad for starters. They got six hundred dollars for the night's work and a telephone call offering them a job in Tampa as opening act for the Ronnies, a successful band that already had an album, *Greatest Hits*, and was already popular in some places, including Wilkes-Barre, Gary, Erie, Louisville, and Baton Rouge. The Ronnies, who were into a combination of punk and heavy metal plus some middle of the road along with jazz, liked some of Trash's music O.K., but they were really turned on by the idea of the chicken bit. When they all met in Tampa to rehearse, the Ronnies cut Trash's set down to three songs and worked up a fifteen-minute routine for the chicken, with strobes and costumes and choreography and a truckload of chicken feathers to dump on the audience at the end. Bobby had to rehearse the chicken bit fourteen times that afternoon, but the Ronnies' manager, a little guy named Darrell Prince, was still not satisfied. Bobby sort of seemed to have lost interest in the whole idea. "I don't know," he said. "I really don't know."

That night, before Trash's first show with the Ronnies, Darrell Prince came up to Don in the dressing room. "You're doing the chicken," he said to him.

"I don't know," Don said. "To tell you the truth, I've never done it before."

"You watched the other kid do it. Just do what he did."

"Well, to be perfectly honest with you, it's not actually something that I am particularly into right now."

"*Get* into it," the guy said, and he talked to Don for several minutes about rock and roll as a ritual expression of tribal unity which sets free powerful feelings, including anger and guilt, that require a blood sacrifice to restore the inner peace and harmony of the tribe. He gave examples of this from Mayan and early Japanese cultures, the Old Testament, NFL Sunday football, and the Spanish Bullring. "Besides," he said, "it's only a chicken."

"I don't know," Don said. "I honestly don't think I could do it that *well*. People pay four, five dollars to get in, they deserve to see a good show. I might just get sick, or something."

But Darrell Prince walked away, and a few minutes later Don and the rest of his friends were standing in a corridor of the amphitheatre ready to go on, and there was another chicken in a cage, and they could all hear the sounds of the crowd, which was already whistling and clapping for them to come out. Don did feel sick, and he didn't know if he was going to be able to do it or not. While he waited, he thought to himself that perhaps by doing it and feeling sick about doing it he would do some good, perhaps by showing any kids that might be in the audience that they should not try to do this, and that maybe it would be an example to them about violence. And besides, that afternoon the *Falling Rocks* story had come out, and they were some sort of stars.

from

ONCE UPON
THE RIVER LOVE

ANDREI MAKINE

Like music, the movies—for better or worse—lay
down a shimmering path out of childhood, even for
those living in the farthest stretches of Siberia. For
the hero of Andrei Makine's novel, a bizarre Jean-
Paul Belmondo film viewed in a remote village not
only opens his mind to the rest of the world, but it
shows him the way out of the taiga.

It was the shark that saved me. . . .

I think if the film had begun differently I would have run out of the cinema and thrown myself under the wheels of the first truck that came by. In the deafening uproar of that brutal engine I would have sought out the blissful silence of the cedar tree. . . .

The film could so easily have begun with a shot of a woman walking through the streets while the credits roll—a woman "walking to meet her destiny." Or with one of a man at the wheel of his car, his impassive face hypnotizing the bemused spectators. Or even with a scenic panorama . . . But it was a shark.

Well, first we saw a man with a shifty face and a shabby light suit. A man trying to call someone from a telephone booth on the sunny promenade of a southern town. He kept glancing around anxiously, cupping his hand over the mouthpiece. He did not have much time. A helicopter appeared in the azure sky. . . . The machine stopped above the phone booth, lowered enormous claws, picked up the booth, and carried it off into the sky. Inside it the wretched spy was shaking the receiver, trying to pass on his ultrasecret message. . . . But the monstrous claws were already opening. The booth fell, plummeted into the sea, landed on the bottom, and there two frogmen secured it very adroitly to a long cage. Using up his last few mouthfuls of air, the spy turned toward the door of the cage. . . . He even managed to draw his pistol and fire. And produced a ridiculous stream of bubbles . . .

A splendid shark, which was, we guessed, ravenously hungry, darted into the submerged booth, pointing its snout at the spy's stomach. The water turned red. . . .

A few moments later Belmondo made his appearance. And the man who was evidently his boss was telling him about his colleague's tragic end. "We succeeded in recovering his remains," he said in very solemn tones. And he showed him a can of . . . shark's fin soup!

It was too silly! Gloriously silly! Completely improbable! Wonderfully crazy!

We had no words to express it. We simply had to accept it and experience it for what it was. Like an existence parallel to our own.

The feature film had been preceded by a newsreel. The three of us were sitting in the front row—the least popular of all, but there were no other seats left when we got there. The voice-over, both ingratiating and hectoring, was pouring out its commentary on the political events of the day. First we saw the imperial splendor of some hall in the Kremlin, where an old man in a dark suit was pinning a medal to the chest of another old man. "In recognition of the merits of Comrade Gromygin toward the fatherland and the people, and his contribution to the cause of international détente, and on the occasion of his seventy-fifth birthday," declaimed the voice-over in ringing tones. And the assembled dark suits began to applaud.

Next appeared a woman in a little polka-dot satin dress who was moving at an incredible speed amid hundreds of bobbins, all turning at maximum velocity. She broke off from her work for a moment just to declare in strident tones: "I'm currently operating a hundred and twenty looms. But to celebrate the seventieth anniversary of our beloved Party, I solemnly resolve to transfer to a hundred and fifty looms." And once again we saw her nimble fingers dancing between the threads and bobbins. Indeed, she now seemed to me to be running from one loom to the next faster than ever, as if she were already preparing to break the record. . . .

The lights came on again before being switched off for the feature film. Samurai nudged me with his elbow and offered me a handful of roasted sunflower seeds. I gripped them in my palm, while remaining in an opaque, all-enveloping torpor. She's going to operate a hundred and fifty looms, I was thinking. Then maybe a hundred and eighty. I sensed that this record-breaking weaver and the splendors of the Kremlin were mysteriously connected both to our dark district center and to the Transsiberian, with that red-haired woman forever waiting for it. . . . I also knew that as soon as the darkness returned I would fling my seeds to the ground and escape to that road shaken by the passage of giant trucks.

Yes, from the moment of those opening scenes, there would be a woman walking to meet her destiny—or a man at the steering wheel of his car. . . .

But it was the shark! The absurdity of the can of fish soup containing the digested mortal remains of the spy was probably the only means by which I could have been kept on the fragile shores of life. Yes, what was needed was precisely that degree of harebrained madness for me to be snatched from reality and catapulted onto that sunny promenade, into that sunken cage where the mind-blowing execution was being prepared. The secret agent devoured by a shark and ending up in a can of fish soup was just what was needed.

And there were also women on that promenade. Above all, those two who for several seconds hid the telephone booth with their miniskirted silhouettes, their indolent bodies, their suntanned legs.

Oh, those divine legs! They moved around on the screen, in time with the sensual, swaying gait of those two shapely young creatures. Tanned thighs that seemed not to have the least idea of the presence, somewhere in the world, of winter, of Nerlug, of our Siberia. Or of the camp whose barbed-wire entanglements had ensnared the sun pendulum. These legs demonstrated with extreme persuasiveness—though without seeking to convert anyone at all—the possibility of an existence without the Kremlin, without weaving looms and other achievements of socialist emulation. Magnificently apolitical thighs. Serenely amoral. Thighs outside History. Apart from all ideology. Without any utilitarian ulterior motive. Thighs for thighs' sake. Quite simply beautiful tanned women's legs!

The shark and the apolitical thighs prepared the way for the appearance of our hero.

He came in many guises, like some Hindu divinity in its infinite incarnations. Now at the wheel of an endless white automobile hurtling into the sea, now making waves in a swimming pool with powerful butterfly strokes, attracting lustful looks from bathing beauties. He demolished his enemies in a thousand ways, fought his way out of the nets they flung over him, rescued his companions in arms. But above all, he seduced unremittingly.

Enthralled, I melted into the multicolored cloud of the screen. So, the woman was not unique!

With unconscious force, I was still gripping the fistful of sunflower seeds. They had become hot, and the blood throbbed in my clenched fist. As if it were my heart I was holding in my hand, so that it should not explode from too much emotion.

It was quite a different heart. Henceforth there was nothing final about the tragic night it had lived through. The red-haired woman's izba was being swiftly transformed, before my very eyes, into just an episode, an experience, one amorous adventure (the first) among many. Under cover of the darkness I turned my head slightly and, furtively, examined

Samurai's and Utkin's profiles. This time I was observing them with a discreet and indulgent smile. With an air of worldly superiority. I felt so much closer to Belmondo than the two of them were, so much better informed about the secrets of feminine sensuality!

And on the screen, in a highly acrobatic but elegant manner, our hero was toppling a superb female spy, in an amorous clinch, onto some piece of furniture that looked quite unsuitable for love. . . . And the tropical night drew a conniving veil over their entwined bodies. . . .

With half-closed eyes, I inhaled deeply exotic scents that tickled the nostrils and made the eyes go misty.

I was saved.

On the whole, we understood little of the universe of Belmondo at the time of that first showing. I do not believe all the plot twists of this farcical parody of spy films could have been accessible to us. Nor the constant shuttling back and forth between the hero, a writer of adventure novels, and his double, the invincible secret agent, thanks to whom the novelist sublimates the miseries and frustrations of his personal life.

We had not grasped this rather obvious device at all. But we perceived the essential: the surprising freedom of this multiple world, where people seemed to escape those implacable laws that ruled our own lives, from the humblest workers' canteen to the imperial hall of the Kremlin, not forgetting the silhouettes of the watchtowers fixed over the camp.

Of course, these extraordinary people had their sufferings and their setbacks too. But the sufferings were not without remedy, and the setbacks stimulated fresh boldness. Their whole lives became an exuberant overreaching of themselves. Muscles were tensed and broke chains, the steely look rebuffed the aggressor; bullets were always delayed for a moment as they nailed the shadows of these leaping beings to the ground.

And Belmondo-the-novelist took this combative freedom to its symbolic apogee: the secret agent's car missed a turn and fell from a clifftop; but the unbridled imagination retrieved it at once by making it go into reverse. In this universe even the step over the brink was not terminal.

Generally the crowd of spectators dispersed quickly after evening performances. They would be in a hurry to dive into a dark alley, go home, get into bed.

This time it was quite different. People emerged slowly, at a sleepwalker's pace, a faint smile on their lips. Spilling out onto a little patch of waste ground behind the cinema, they spent a moment marking time, blinded, deafened. Intoxicated. They exchanged smiles. Strangers paired off, formed unaccustomed, fleeting circles, as in a very slow, agreeably irregular dance. And the stars in the milder sky seemed larger, closer.

It was under this light, less cold than before, that we walked along those little twisting alleys that had been reduced to narrow passageways between mountains of snow. We were on our way to the house of Utkin's grandfather, who let us stay in his big izba on our visits to the city.

Walking along Indian file in the depths of this maze of snow, we were silent. The universe we had just been exposed to remained, for the moment, beyond words. All there was to express it was the languid beauty of the night of the thaw, the quiet breathing of the taiga, these close stars, the denser color of the sky and the more vivid tones of the snows. But we could still only sense it in our flesh, in the quivering of our nostrils, in our young bodies, which drank in both the starry sky and the scents of the taiga. Filled to the brim with this new universe, we carried it in silence, afraid of spilling its magical contents. Only a repressed sigh escaped occasionally to convey this overload of emotions: "Belmondo . . ."

It was in Utkin's grandfather's izba that the eruption took place. We all began shouting at the same time, waving our arms and leaping around, each eager to portray the film in the most lively manner. We roared, as we struggled in the nets flung by our enemies; we snatched the glamorous creature from the sadistic clutches of the executioners as they prepared to cut off one of her breasts; we machine-gunned the walls before rolling onto a divan. We were at one and the same time the spy in the telephone booth and the shark pointing its aggressive snout, and even the can of fish soup!

We were transformed into a pyrotechnic display of gestures, grimaces, and yells. We were discovering the ineffable language of our new universe. That of Belmondo!

In any other circumstance, Utkin's grandfather, a man with the corpulence of a weary and melancholy giant, whose slow gait and white hair made him reminiscent of a polar bear, would have quickly rebuked us. But on this occasion he watched our triple performance in silence. The three of us together must have succeeded in re-creating the atmosphere of the film. Yes, he must have pictured the underground labyrinth lit by the dismal flames of torches, and the wall to which the glamorous martyr was chained. He saw a monstrous figure, squat and shriveled, cackling with perverse and impotent lust, as he drew closer to his scantily clad victim and raised a pitilessly glittering blade over her delectable breast. But a mingled roar came from our three outraged throats. The hero, triple in his strength and beauty, flexed his muscles, broke the chains, and flew to the aid of the gorgeous prisoner. . . .

The polar bear screwed up his eyes mischievously and left the room.

Samurai and I broke off our theatricals, thinking we had really offended Grandfather too much. Only Utkin remained in his actor's trance, shuddering as if it were he who risked losing a breast.

Grandfather reappeared in the room, grasping the neck of a bottle of champagne with his great knotty fingers. My eyes opened wide. Samurai uttered a resounding "Aha!" And Utkin emerged from his epileptic fit and summed up all our emotions in a single exclamation, still talking about the film: "Well, that's the West for you!"

Grandfather put three chipped china cups and a thick glass tumbler on the table.

"I've been saving this bottle for a friend," he explained, liberating the cork from the wire top. "But he, poor fellow, had the odd idea of dying in the meantime. He was a friend from the front. . . ."

We hardly heard his explanations. The cork leaped out with a joyful crack, there was a moment of cheerful urgency— abundant froth, fierce popping of bubbles, a white surge spilling onto the tablecloth. And finally the first mouthful of champagne, the very first in our lives . . .

It was only years later, thanks to that bitter clarification of the past that comes with age, that we would remember the friend from the front. . . . But on that evening of the thaw long ago there was only this icy tickling inside our scorched throats, which caused tears of joy to well up. A happy weariness like that of actors after a first night. And Utkin's summary, still ringing in our ears: "Well, that's the West for you!"

Yes, the Western World was born in the sparkle of Crimean

champagne, in the middle of a big izba buried in the snow after a French film several years old.

It was the Western World at its most authentic, because engendered in vitro. In that thick glass tumbler that had been washed by whole waves of vodka. And also in our virgin imaginations. In the crystalline purity of the air of the taiga.

It was there, the West. And that night we dreamed of it with open eyes in the bluish darkness of the izba. . . . And three shadowy figures appeared on that southern promenade, whom the summer visitors certainly will not have noticed. These three figures walked around a telephone booth, strolled past a café terrace, and, with their timid gaze, followed two young creatures with beautiful tanned legs. . . .

Our first steps in the Western World.

We were flying through the taiga, stretched out along the trunks of cedar trees on the trailer of a powerful tractor, like those that carried rockets in the army. The rough bark under our backs, the sky sparkling above our eyes, the silvery shadows of the forest on either side of the road. The sunny air inflated our sheepskin coats like sails and shot us through with the smell of resin.

It was strictly forbidden to transport people on trailers, especially when loaded. But the driver had accepted us with cheerful nonchalance. It was the first sign of the changes brought into our existence by Belmondo. . . .

The window of the cabin was lowered, so soft did the air seem that morning. And all along the road we could hear the driver telling the story of the film to his passenger, the foreman of the loggers. Lying flat out on the trees, we followed his narration, delivered with exclamations, oaths, and broad gestures, as his hands perilously left the steering wheel.

From time to time he uttered a particularly ringing cry. "He's got his first tooth, my boy! Ha ha ha! You know what I mean? That's it. My wife wrote to me. . . ."

And he resumed his narrative: "So then he pulls on the chains with all his strength, like that. . . . Sure thing, you could hear his bones cracking. Wow! And bingo! he chucks them in the air. And the other one, with his blade, was just a couple of steps away from the girl. And she—I can't tell you what a great pair of tits she's got. And this bastard wants to cut one of them off. You know what I mean? So the guy goes in right under him and ker-pow! No, no, don't worry. I'm holding the wheel."

And again he interrupted his story to proclaim his fatherly pride: "Hey, the little rascal! His first tooth . . . Milka writes: 'I can't feed him anymore—he bites my breast till it bleeds.' Ha ha ha! He's just like his dad."

The world seemed wonderfully transfigured. All we needed was a miracle to be finally convinced of it. And the miracle came.

It was close to the Devil's Bend, even more dangerous

under the drifts from the snowstorm. At the place where we should have been moving cautiously, making a slow descent to the bank of the Olyei. But the story was reaching its culmination. . . .

The tractor with its heavy trailer hurtled down the slope, without even slowing down, and plunged out over the thin ice undermined by warm springs. . . .

There was a yell, quickly stifled, from inside the cabin; an oath uttered by Samurai. And then several apocalyptic and interminable seconds, filled with the creaking of the ice giving way under the wheels . . .

We came to ourselves a hundred yards farther along, already on the other bank. The driver stopped the engine and jumped out into the snow. His passenger followed him. The white surface of the river was incised by two black tracks that were slowly filling with water. . . .

In the absolute silence, nothing could be heard but a faint whistling coming from the engine. The sky had quite a new sparkle to it.

Later, no doubt, the driver and the foreman would talk about a crazy stroke of luck. Or about the speed of the tractor, which had been flying along, scarcely touching the ground. But without their admitting it to themselves, the ruins of the church on the highest part of the riverbank would come into their minds. And without knowing how to think about it, let alone talk about it, they would muse on that remote childish presence (the first tooth!). Maybe this had mysteriously sustained the heavy machine as it crossed the fragile ice. . . .

But we preferred to believe in a simple miracle; from now on this would be so natural in our lives.

On my return, everything in our izba seemed strange to me. It was the strangeness of familiar objects staring at me with curiosity; they seemed to be waiting for my first move. The day before yesterday I had left that room in the morning, to go to school. Since then there had been the switch operator's shanty; the station waiting room; the snowstorm; the house of the red-haired woman; the bridge; the truckdriver. . . . I shook my head, overcome with a singular dizziness. Yes, then my return across the snow-filled valley, the rusty nails of the hanged men . . .

My aunt came in, carrying the big kettle.

"I've made some pancakes, but some of them are burned; you can leave those," she said in her most normal voice, putting on the table a plate with a pile of golden pancakes.

I looked at this woman in perplexity. There she was entering the room, and she was coming from quite a different era. From before the snowstorm . . . Suddenly I remembered that there had been the sunny promenade beside the sea, the shark, the underground chamber with the chained beauty . . . I felt myself reeling. Without explaining anything to my aunt, I left the room and pushed open the front door.

The evening sun was drowsing behind the castellated

skyline of the taiga, caught in the watchtowers' invisible trap. Thanks to the purplish haze from the mild spell, you could stare at the coppery disk without screwing up your eyes. And the disk, I was sure, was swaying slightly above the barbed wire. . . .

Next day when Samurai knocked on our door and said to me with a wink: "Let's go!" there was no mistaking what he proposed.

We put on our snowshoes, collected Utkin close by his izba, and left Svetlaya. . . .

The city, twenty-three miles by road, was nineteen if you cut through the taiga. Eight hours on the march, plus a couple of stops to have a bite to eat and especially to give Utkin a breather. An entire day's journey. At the end of it: a sunset and the mists of the city that lay between two arms of the taiga, where it opened out gradually. And closer and closer came the hour, which each time became more magical: six-thirty p.m. The evening performance. Belmondo's.

Already the dense taiga was opening out; our snowy road was leading us straight to that promenade beside the sea and into the midst of that tanned crowd of extraterrestrials in the Western World. . . .

The first time, we had understood little. And indeed, there were things in the film it was hard for us to comprehend.

The character of the publisher, for example. His relationship with our hero was an absolute mystery to us. Why was Belmondo afraid of this obese, inelegant man who hid his baldness under a wig? What dominion could he exercise over our superman and by what right? How dared he carelessly cast aside the manuscript that our hero brought him in his office?

For want of any credible explanation, we concluded it was sexual rivalry. And indeed, the hero's lovely neighbor was the target of repeated assaults by this monstrous literary bureaucrat. The whole audience held its breath when, drooling with lust, he feasted his prying eyes on the delectable backside of the young woman as she rashly leaned a little too far over the desk. And it was he who later pounced on the unfortunate woman, scattering his thick-lipped kisses all over her body when her defenses were down as a result of a treacherous drugged cigarette. . . .

Many of the nuances in this film escaped us. But thanks to our sixth sense, as young savages from the taiga, we could perceive intuitively what intellectually we could not know about the lives of Westerners. And we had decided to see the film ten or twenty times over if need be, but to understand everything! Everything down to the detail that tortured us for several days: when the lovely creature called on our hero, who was evidently a most welcoming host, why did she refuse his offer of a glass of whiskey?

from

SEX AND DEATH TO THE AGE 14

SPALDING GRAY

Getting your driver's license is one of the few offi-
cially defined moments of maturity. Car-obsessed
Spalding Gray, though, did not wait for government
sanction before he got behind the wheel and in
this selection shows what can happen when
you learn too much too soon.

My father owned a '54 two-tone gray and royal blue Ford. It had an automatic transmission, which made it difficult to spin the wheel unless you could find a patch of sand. Then, if you put it in low and floored it, it would leave a small strip. I didn't have my driver's license, but I loved to drive and would often ask my mother if I could go park the car in the garage. I would go out and sit in the car, put on my sunglasses and just rev the engine until I felt like James Dean in *Giant*. Then I would drive all over the neighborhood waving to friends and neighbors, looking for patches of sand where I could spin the wheels.

My mother asked me if I wanted to go see *East of Eden* and I said, "No. I don't want to see any more Bible stories." Shortly after that, James Dean was killed when his Porsche Spyder hit a Ford sedan driven by a man named Turnupseed. My mother lamented the loss of the man. She said, "We've lost a great actor." I felt sorry for the car. The Porsche Spyder was my favorite. The picture of his mangled car was displayed in all the driver ed classes in California. I saw the photo in a magazine in the Rexall drugstore at the Barrington shopping center.

When I was 15 I wanted to become a driver for the Ferrari team. That's what I wanted to be when I grew up. I wanted to be like the Marquis de Portago, the Italian who raced for the

Ferrari team. He was the one who put an end to the *mille-meglia* when his car had a blowout at 130 miles a hour, killing seven people. I saw the picture of the bodies flying through the air in *Life* magazine. He was a very handsome man. There was also a picture of the marquis kissing his girlfriend, who was an American movie star. And under the picture was a caption, "I make love every night and I'm not ashamed to admit it." Every night, God, that was incredible to me then. I was a virgin at the time, and I just couldn't imagine it.

The Marquis de Portago was my distant hero, but at home it was Donny Renshaw. We called him Donny Duals because he had dual exhausts on his car. I'm not saying that was unusual—so did Oldsmobiles, Cadillacs, and Pontiacs at that time—but he had dual straight pipes. No muffler. Donny had a '40 Ford coupe with patches of primer on it, dual carburetors, and a radical cam that made the whole thing rough-idle like a John Deere tractor about to stall out.

When he geared down on Rumstick Road, I'd jump up and run to my window. It was like the call of the wild. Also, Donny had dropped out of school to become a steeplejack and the thought of him up there on that white, pointed Congregational Church steeple just hanging there, jacking, was too much. I mean, he was a saint to me, a poet. When he wasn't up there, he was just driving the car up and down Rumstick Road, and then at 10 o'clock in the morning, while we were in high school, he would pull in, pull a U-y in front of the Automobile Mechanics Course garage, lay a strip and roar back out. And I thought, that's what I want to do when I'm 16. The only problem was I had vertigo, so I didn't know about the steeplejack stuff, but I was definitely going to get one of those cars.

Now Donny Duals was the local hero; we couldn't get close to him. We never saw him outside of his car, except once when it was in the shop. He was walking up Rumstick Road and my brothers and I went across the street to get a closer look. My younger brother Chan had a cap gun that Donny grabbed out of his hand and my older brother Rocky said, "Hey, come on. Give him a break, he's just a little kid. Have a heart." And Donny goes like this, "Yeah, sure, great. Ya got one?"

At the time I was learning how to drive without my driver's license. I was learning how to drive like an old woman with my Gram Gray in her '48 Chevy stick shift down on Half-Mile Road.

I was also learning how to drive on my own. I had always wanted a '40 Ford coupe. Other than the '32 Ford coupe, the '40 was one of the most sought-after cars around. Once when my parents were away on a ski trip in Vermont, Spike Claxton and I happened to be over in Bay Springs and spotted one just parked in a driveway. It didn't have a for sale sign on it, but I thought we should make an offer anyway. When we knocked on the door of the house an old man answered, and I just offered him $75 cash for the car. I had two paper routes at the time—a morning route and an evening one—and $75 was all I'd saved up from both of them. When the man said yes, I just rushed off to my bank, took out all my savings, and bought the car.

Then a strange thing happened, a strange thing that felt like a dream. The owner, perhaps because he was so happy to get all that money for such a piece of junk, just left his plates on the car and let me drive it away. Spike and I just took that car and drove it all over town. We even drove it up to Providence and around Blackstone Boulevard, then back to Barrington, and then up to Providence again. I parked it in my yard and just looked at it. It was so beautiful I couldn't stand it. I knew I had to find a place for it before the weekend was over because my parents were coming home. So at last I moved it, knocking down some of the rose bushes, along the edge of our garage and parked it next to the little shack my brother Rocky had built when he wanted to become a Maine guide.

My parents were very upset when they came home and saw all the squashed rose bushes and this '40 Ford, which looked like a piece of junk, sitting in their backyard. We had a big fight. "What are you going to do with it?" they asked. I told them that I was going to fix it up, rebuild the engine, and convert it into a perfect street-rod. I think they wanted to believe me. They wanted to think that this would be a worthy endeavor, a wholesome activity to keep me off the streets.

So, with the help of some friends, I did get the engine out. I got it down into our basement and tore it apart. I got all the valves and pistons removed and then I got bored and just left it there. I couldn't stand the constant grease on my hands. I had seen the insides of that engine and that was enough. It was then that I knew I didn't want to be an automobile mechanic.

I don't remember what happened to that engine block, but I sold the body of the car to Jeff Howe for $35 and he had it towed back out over the rose bushes, dropped a four-barrel '57 Chevy engine in it, and made himself a fine street-rod. I looked the other way every time it passed. I was keeping in touch with my racecar driving at Seekonk Speedway, a quarter-mile stockcar track in Massachusetts, where all these incredibly fast and loud cars went around in circles. They had no mufflers at all and you could hear the sound and see the searchlights from the speedway 10 miles away. A bunch of us would go up there early, just as the sun was going down, build a ladder out of fallen trees and climb up over the fence to get in free so we could have money to buy beer.

I first practiced driving on the clamshell driveway out behind our house on Rumstick Road. That driveway was only about 40 feet long, so there was no chance of getting up much speed, and since I didn't have my driver's license I couldn't continue out onto the street. Because of this, most of the practice consisted of "backing and filling," until one day a bunch of us got carried away and just had an orgy of spinning wheels. I made that family car spin and dig, while my friends looked on and cheered, until the clamshell driveway looked like Normandy Beach after the invasion. And in the middle of almost destroying the entire driveway, we were interrupted with a quasi citizen's arrest by Desmond Musgrove from next door. Desmond was slightly retarded and thought he was a cop. He had a big Schwinn bicycle and would ride around town talking into his hand like it was a CB radio. It was difficult to tell his age, but he was a big guy, not to be fooled with. Anyway, he came over and put a quick stop to it all. He even tried to fingerprint us with his official True Detective G-Man Fingerprint Kit.

The other clamshell driveway where I practiced was at Craig Crane's in Bristol, Rhode Island, and that was more spectacular. His parents had this fantastic mile-long clamshell driveway at the end of Papasquash Point, and Ryan, Craig, and I used it as a race track. So that he wouldn't wreck their car, Craig's parents bought him a '49 Packard convertible with overdrive and also a little lever you could throw to convert it from hydraulic shift into standard. None of us had our driver's license yet, so we'd just drive Craig's Packard up and down that mile-long clamshell driveway. The only problem, as Ryan saw it, was that the Packard wasn't loud enough. Ryan was obsessed with what we called "highway sounds." So was I, in fact, and so was Scott Tarbox. We picked "highway sounds" up from the Chuck Berry 45 single "Maybelline."

Ryan knew how to make fabulous highway sounds with his mouth. Ryan, Scott, and I would sit around drinking vanilla Cokes at the Rexall drugstore and Scott would say, "Hey, Moe," (he called Ryan "Moe") "I'll pay you a nickel to make a highway sound." And Ryan, just sitting there on a stool, would put his mouth into gear and let out with these incredible rapping highway sounds. Saliva flying everywhere. Scott would go wild and say, "Do it again, Moe, only this time don't use the clutch. Just slam shift through the gears!" Then Scott would up the fee and pay him a dime for slam-shifting this time, and Ryan would make the sound. After that we'd wander out and lean against the drugstore and talk about the cars driving in and out of the shopping center.

On rainy days we'd sit around and listen to recordings of road races. I had all the records with the best highway sounds. I had "The Sounds of Seabring," "Sounds from Watkins Glen," and best of all, a recording of Le Mans on which we could listen to a real Le Mans start, where the drivers would have to run from a starting line, jump in their cars, and start them up. Then there was this thunderous noise of all the cars pealing rubber as they took off.

Another favorite record was "Pit Stop"—you could hear

the drivers talk when they pulled in for repairs. You could hear the actual voices of Phil Hill, Juan Manuel Fangio, Porfirio Rubirosa, and Wolfgang von Tripps, who was eventually killed in a race. After that happened, my brother Rocky, who had just found out about existentialism, said that it wasn't really a meaningless death because Wolfgang was doing exactly what he wanted when he died. Not to have raced would have made him something else, something other than a racecar driver. I thought I understood.

Well, we'd sit around and listen to "Sounds from Watkins Glen" and hear all the men talk so that we could pick up on the actual lingo:

> "Well, what's going on here anyway? Well, what's going on, it looks like we're having some technical inspection."
>
> "Did you get my car through inspection?"
>
> "Yeah, it's all done."
>
> "You mean you actually got it through this time? How many times did you have to go back?"
>
> "Well, that's pretty good, that's par for the course."
>
> "What was wrong with it?"
>
> "Uh, a toe rim on the rear wheel."
>
> "Toe rim on the rear wheel, okay, well I never heard of that either. Probably their machine."

"Probably."

"On the rear wheel alignment—there *is* no alignment on the rear wheels."

"The only thing that could happen is if there's a bent axle or something of that nature."

"A bent wheel might do it. Other than that there's no adjustment for it."

"There's no toe in and no toe out."

"We could have a bent bell housing as well, slightly bent over there."

"That's unlikely though."

"Hey, what do we have here? This is George Hansen, he's an old Jaguar driver. I think we might call George Mr. Jaguar. One of the oldest Jaguar drivers, not in age, not in age, but in the length of time driving Jaguars. Recently George graduated from a production class. And now he runs a one-forty, excuse me, he *used* to run a one-twenty, he now has a . . . and he's gonna run that up here. . . ."

But Craig's Packard did not make the kind of highway sounds Ryan wanted to hear, so whenever Craig was inside watching soap operas (which was often), Ryan would go under Craig's car with a little ax and chop some holes in his muffler, then he'd ask Craig to come out and do a test drive around the yard. And Craig would do it, he'd act dumb and say, "Hey guys, what do you want me to do that for?" And Ryan would just say, "Go on and do it. Just give it a try." So Craig would drive it around the circle in front of his house and then go back in to watch TV. And Ryan would crawl under the car and give the muffler a few more whacks. This went on for a period of time, until Craig's Packard finally sounded like it needed a new muffler.

Craig was very possessive of his Packard and would rarely let us drive it. I really wanted my own car to race on his clamshell driveway, so I bought a '37 Plymouth for $35. I bought it in Barrington and drove it unregistered, without a license, down to Bristol. The windshield opened with a little crank and we let the fresh air blow in. Ryan rode shotgun and kept an eye out for cops. It was a very exciting trip. When we got to Bristol, we took the side route to Craig's along Colt's Drive, a semiprivate winding road that used to belong to the Colt estate along the edges of Narragansett Bay. It wound around like a racetrack road and we took those corners like we were in a Ferrari.

When we got to Craig's, the first thing Ryan did was to crawl under the Plymouth and rip off the entire exhaust system. Off came the muffler and off came the tail pipe. Then we bought a piece of flex-pipe at Western Auto and attached it, so it was running directly off the manifold and back out under the running board. And we were off. It was fantastic! It sounded like the whole of Seekonk Speedway on a Saturday night.

Craig's parents owned a hundred acres of land, so there was no one around to complain, and we'd just drive that Plymouth up and down the clamshell driveway, slam-shifting through the gears as flames shot out the straight pipe under the door. Then I'd let Ryan take it for a spin, and spin is what we'd do. Oh how we'd spin. We'd get it to the top of the driveway and then gun it, and drive it flat out until we reached the right-angle turn at the bottom, and we'd go into that turn at full-tilt boogie. The car would slide off the clamshell, spin almost full circle, bounce through some trees, squash some skunk cabbage, and then, with the help of my plastic suicide knob with the naked lady on it, I'd manage to get it all back on the track.

At night it was even better because you could see the orange flames shoot out from under the door. Life could have stopped there, but it didn't.

At last I turned 16 and it was time to get my driver's license. I couldn't wait. This meant that I'd be "street legal" and out on the highways. I'd even be able to drive to Boston if I wanted to. Ryan couldn't wait either because he wasn't 16 yet. I knew I was a good driver and that I'd have no trouble with the road test. So I went up on my birthday, June 5, to take the test, but the one thing that I didn't do was study the driver's manual hard enough. And I failed the written test. I couldn't believe it. I passed the road test with flying colors, but I failed the written test. I was so mortified that when I got home I lied to Ryan. I told him I was caught cheating, because I'd much rather have been thought a cheater than a cretin. The following week, after endless late-night study of the driver's manual, I went back to Providence and passed the test.

Now I was on the road and could really practice in the family car, my father's gray and royal blue two-tone '54 Ford, and that car did not have what I would call a low center of gravity. It was nothing like a Ferrari. But that didn't stop me. I was off. And the first mishap I had was at Barrington Beach. This was what I would have to call an unconscious mistake. It had nothing to do with racing.

One day I was just driving down the hill to the town beach, and instead of turning left to park in the lot with all the other cars, I drove straight out onto the beach and toward the bay. I don't know what got into me that day. Just before reaching the bay, the car sunk down in the sand and stopped, and I just sat there spinning the wheels. As I sat there I could see that the tide was coming in and that the car would soon fill up with water. I jumped out of the car and ran to the pay phone to call a tow truck, and they got it out just as the water reached the front wheels. The brake drums were filled with sand and the car had to go into the shop to have them cleaned. My father didn't seem all that upset. He just couldn't figure out why I would have done a stupid thing like that. And I was no help.

Both my parents dealt with my automotive mishaps very

well. They never seemed to get rattled. Once I had to appear in the traffic court in Providence and my mother had to accompany me. It was a snowy day and we were driving down this big hill leading into town when someone put on their brakes way up ahead of us. When I saw his brake lights go on, I hit my brakes and Mom and I just sat there while our car slid out of control and bumped into his. There was no apparent damage, but I'm sure he was crying "whiplash." Mom just said, "Step it up, Spuddy dear. Do the best you can." I just pulled out around his car as Mom rolled down her window and called out, "Sorry, this kind of weather, you know."

After the Ford got out of the shop, I tried to drive more carefully. I was sure the Marquis de Portago would never get stuck in the sand. My next big mishap took place on Colt's Drive. Colt's Drive had become my favorite practice spot, and Larry Lindberger had become my new copilot. One rainy September day when I was going through my laps, the car slid sideways on some wet leaves just before the stone bridge. Larry was impressed. Back on the road again I hit another patch of leaves at the corner by the playground and the car went into a full skid and rolled. I don't remember anything after that until I came to. When I did come to, I found that the car was teetering on its side on the small sea wall, just inches away from falling into the bay. And Larry was using my body as a ladder to climb out the passenger door, which he'd pried open above us like a hatch. The radio was playing "The Girl Can't Help It" full blast, and the first thing I did was to reach over and turn it off. Then, following Larry, I climbed out. We just stood there in the rain, looking at the chassis of the rolled Ford. Larry turned to me and said, "If my mother knew I was out here in the rain with this sore throat she'd kill me." And I thought, oh God, Larry's in shock. Then he turned to me and said, "Shit man, you're a mess. You've got blood pouring down your face." It was then that I realized that I was also in shock.

We walked together in a daze up Colt's Drive until we reached the National Guard Headquarters and I called Gram Gray to come pick us up while one of the National Guardsmen called the Silver Tow Truck Service.

Mom broke the news to Dad when he got home that night. I was upstairs in bed, depressed, with a bad stiff neck. I couldn't move my head in any direction. After Mom told Dad, he drove down to Bristol to examine the wreck. When he got back, Mom asked him how it looked, and he said, "Like the two boys inside it should have been killed." And at first I wasn't sure if he meant that we should be dead because of what we did, or dead from the crash. But I figured he must have meant the crash because the side of the car had been ripped apart by the sea wall and it looked like a can of Dinty Moore someone had opened with a Swiss army knife.

I was depressed for days and didn't want to drive anymore. Once again I couldn't understand why Dad wasn't angry. He just seemed to accept it. I didn't miss any school, and the following day I found out that everyone knew about the accident because a photo of the car had appeared in the *Providence Journal.* There it was, on its side, teetering on the edge of the sea wall. The photo had been taken straight on, so that the license plate was clearly visible. No mistaking whose car it was: G914, the Gray's of Barrington, Rhode Island.

The first thing that happened when I got into school the next morning was that Mr. Bender, the driver ed teacher, called me into his room for a private chat. I don't think Mr. Bender liked me all that much. One of the reasons for this was that I wasn't a good student; the other was that I'd learned how to drive with my grandmother instead of him. Also, by now there were rumors going around school that Larry Lindberger was either dead or in the hospital. It turned out that Larry *did* have a sore throat after all and the day after the accident he came down with the Asian flu. So he was at home in bed.

I think Larry got better in about two weeks. I never saw much of him after that. Between the accident, the way he used to treat his parakeet, and the fact that his father bought him my Gram Gray's '48 Chevy, things were never the same. That was the car I had learned to drive in and I couldn't stand seeing Larry drive it. It wasn't just that he had his own car and I had none. It was the fact that as soon as he got the car, he put Hollywood mufflers on it, lowered the rear, and hung fuzzy dice and a pink chiffon scarf from the rearview mirror. And in the morning he'd just sit there in that transformed car, just sit out there in his driveway, warming it up, revving the engine for the big five-minute drive to school, while I walked.

So Mr. Bender just took me in his back office and didn't say a word about the accident. He just sat me down and told me a little story. He said, "You know, your Grandfather Horton is a fine upstanding man. Once when he was at a basketball game that I was coaching, he left early and accidentally sideswiped my car, which was parked out front. And he left a note on the windshield that read 'Elmer S. Horton did this.' Then he left his phone number at the bottom of the note. He is a fine upstanding man and you will never turn out like that." That was all he said.

My Gramp Horton *was* a fine upstanding man and he really knew how to take care of his cars. He would buy a new black Mercury with red upholstery every three years. He knew exactly when to buy and sell so he'd get his money's worth. He'd cover his seats with plastic so they wouldn't get warm. In fact, I used to think his cars were in better shape when he traded them in than when he bought them. Gramp was in advertising and knew all about planned obsolescence. But still, there was something about his immaculate cars that Rocky, Chan, and I just couldn't stand and we'd love it when something went wrong. Like the time Teddy Hike threw up from too many pink Canadian mints in the back seat on the way home from Sunday School. My grandfather seemed more upset about the throwup on the back seat than he did about Teddy being sick. That used to drive me and my brothers wild.

I remember the best joke we played on him. Once when Gram and Gramp Horton came to visit, Rocky and I took one of the fake dog shits that came in a box labeled "Doggie Done-It." It was made of rubber and really looked like a big fresh dog shit. The only thing missing was the smell. We took that "Doggie Done-It" and put it right on my grandfather's front seat, and when he came out of the house and discovered it we thought he was going to have a heart attack. His whole face turned red and the veins popped out from his neck as he cried out to Gram Horton, "Peg, come quick! The cat's been here. The cat's been in here!" Rocky, Chan, and I laughed and laughed. We laughed until we couldn't stand it anymore. It wasn't so much Gramp's face we were laughing at as the idea of a cat being able to take a shit that big.

Insurance paid for the '54 Ford to be fixed, and it was back on the road in a matter of weeks. As for myself, I just stayed away from driving for a while. I wasn't so sure about becoming a member of the Ferrari team after all. But then suddenly everything changed. Out of the blue, Dad decided to up and buy an Austin Healy. I couldn't believe it. It was like Walter Mitty had come alive and was working out his major fantasy. I had always known that Dad was interested in Austin Healys, but I never thought he'd really buy one. Then one Saturday he asked me if I wanted to drive up to Preston Auto, the foreign car place in Seekonk. On the spot, he bought one, this beautiful jet black, secondhand Austin Healy with red bucket seats. He bought it right there and together we drove it home.

When we got home the whole neighborhood came out to see us drive in. It was like a for-real pit stop, right there in Barrington, Rhode Island. Everyone wanted a test ride and Dad began to drive them one at a time, down Chapin Road, along the river and then back. At last I asked if I could take Judy Griggs for a ride and he said, "Yes, you may." I was trembling all over. So I drove Judy down along the river and around the back to the waiting crowd at the finish line. As I pulled in, smoke was pouring off the rear tires. I had forgotten to take off the emergency brake and the rear brake drums were almost in flames. Watching the red paint peel off those drums beneath the chrome spokes, I knew my racing career was over.

from

GROWING UP

RUSSELL BAKER

Pulitzer Prize–winning columnist Russell Baker had
no clue what he wanted to do with his life as a boy;
no lifelong dreams, no particular thing he wanted
to be when he grew up. This chapter from his best-
selling memoir tells of the glorious stretch when he
finally discovered what he was good at.

"Something will come along."

That became my mother's battle cry as I plowed into the final year of high school. Friends began asking her what Russell planned to do when he graduated, and her answer was, "Something will come along." She didn't know what, and nothing was in sight on the horizon, but she'd survived so long now on faith that something always came along for people who did their best. "Russ hasn't made up his mind yet, but something will come along," she told people.

I saw no possibilities and looked forward to the end of school days with increasing glumness. It was assumed I would get a job. Boys of our economic class didn't ordinarily go to college. My education, however, hadn't fitted me for labor. While I was reading the Romantic poets and learning Latin syntax, practical boys had been taking shop, mechanical drawing, accounting, and typing. I couldn't drive a nail without mashing my thumb. When I mentioned my inadequacies to my mother she said, "Something will come along, Buddy."

If, gloomily, I said, "Fat chance," she snapped at me, "For God's sake, Russell, have a little gumption. Look on the bright side."

I didn't mind the prospect of working. Having worked since I was eight, I had acquired the habit of work, but I was stymied about what kind of full-time work I might be fit for. That winter I was trying to muster enthusiasm for a career in the grocery business. Moving from Lombard Street to Marydell Road, I had lost my newspaper route. To make up the lost income I'd taken a Saturday job at a large grocery in the Hollins Market, which paid $14 for twelve hours' work. It was a "self-service" store, a primitive forerunner of the supermarket, the first expression of an idea whose time had not yet come. Situated in a dilapidated old building where groceries had once been sold, old-style, across the counter, it bore little resemblance to the bulging supermonuments to consumption that were to rise after World War II. There was no air-conditioning in summer and little heat in winter. Under the cellar's cobwebbed rafters an occasional rat scurried among sacks of cornmeal and hundred-pound bags of flour. As a stock clerk, I toted merchandise from the cellar, marked its price in black crayon, and stacked it on shelves for Saturday shoppers. The flour sacks were slung over the shoulder and lugged upstairs to be dipped from with an aluminum scoop on demand.

The manager was Mr. Simmons, a bawdy, exuberant slave driver who had learned the business in the days of over-the-counter selling, when a manager's personality could attract customers or turn them away. Simmons was a tall, square-shouldered man who affected the breezy style, as though he'd studied his trade under burlesque comedians.

His head was as round and hairless as a cannon ball. He wore big horn-rimmed glasses and bow ties, and his mouth, which was wide and frequently open from ear to ear, displayed dazzling rows of teeth so big they would have done credit to a horse.

Throughout the day the store was filled with his roars, guffaws, shouted jokes, and curses. He romped the aisles in a Groucho Marx lope, administering tongue lashings when he discovered empty shelves where the canned tomatoes or the Post Toasties or the Ovaltine were supposed to be. Spotting a handsome woman at the meat counter, he might glide behind the hamburger grinder to whisper sotto voce some dirty joke at the butcher's ear, then glare at the woman, part his mouth from ear to ear, and display his magnificent ivory. The store was his stage, and he treated it as if he were its star, director, producer, and owner.

If there was a dull half hour he might creep up behind one of the stock clerks hoisting oatmeal from crate to shelf, goose him with both thumbs, then gallop away roaring with laughter. Many of the customers were black and poor and arrived late on Saturday nights hoping to have their paychecks cashed. With them Simmons played Simon Legree, examining their checks suspiciously, demanding identification papers, then rejecting some damp proffered document as inadequate. "That damn thing is so dirty I don't even want to touch it. You open it up and show it to me." Or, if the credentials were in order: "I don't know whether I'm going to cash this check or not. How much do you want to buy here?"

Simmons boasted of being a great lecher. In the cellar ceiling he had drilled a small hole through which he could look up the skirts of women customers standing at the cash register overhead. When a woman who pleased his fancy entered the store, he ostentatiously departed for the cellar with some such cry as "Hot damn! I've got to see more of this." Rolling his eyeballs and smacking his lips he plunged into the cellar and could be found there standing on a pile of flour sacks, one eye glued to his peephole.

I wasn't exhilarated by the grocery business, but at least I was getting experience I thought might help me get full-time work at it after high school. For this purpose I wanted to learn to work the cash register so I could become a checker, the most glamorous job in the store except for the manager's. Simmons withheld this prize. At some point I'd made the mistake of trying to show him I was fancily educated, thinking this would move him to promote me from cellar labor. Whether he took me for an overeducated young fool or whether he resented my failure to laugh loudly enough at his jokes, I don't know. Whatever the reason, I waited in vain for my chance to work the cash register. I knew I would never get it when Simmons, desperate one day for help at the cash registers, came down to the cellar, passed me by, and called on Earl to do the job. Earl was black, and black people were contemptible to Simmons but still preferable to me. It made me wonder if I was cut out for the grocery business. But on the other hand, what else was there?

The only thing that truly interested me was writing, and I knew that sixteen-year-olds did not come out of high school and become writers. I thought of writing as something to be done only by the rich. It was so obviously not real work, not a job at which you could earn a living. Still, I had begun to think of myself as a writer. It was the only thing for which I seemed to have the smallest talent, and, silly though it sounded when I told people I'd like to be a writer, it gave me a way of thinking about myself which satisfied my need to have an identity.

The notion of becoming a writer had flickered off and on in my head since the Belleville days, but it wasn't until my third year in high school that the possibility took hold. Until then I'd been bored by everything associated with English courses. I found English grammar dull and baffling. I hated the assignments to turn out "compositions," and went at them like heavy labor, turning out leaden, lackluster paragraphs that were agonies for teachers to read and for me to write. The classics thrust on me to read seemed as deadening as chloroform.

When our class was assigned to Mr. Fleagle for third-year English I anticipated another grim year in that dreariest of subjects. Mr. Fleagle was notorious among City students for dullness and inability to inspire. He was said to be stuffy, dull, and hopelessly out of date. To me he looked to be sixty or seventy and prim to a fault. He wore primly severe eyeglasses, his wavy hair was primly cut and primly combed. He wore prim vested suits with neckties blocked primly against the collar buttons of his primly starched white shirts. He had a primly pointed jaw, a primly straight nose, and a prim manner of speaking that was so correct, so gentlemanly, that he seemed a comic antique.

I anticipated a listless, unfruitful year with Mr. Fleagle and for a long time was not disappointed. We read *Macbeth*. Mr. Fleagle loved *Macbeth* and wanted us to love it too, but he lacked the gift of infecting others with his own passion. He tried to convey the murderous ferocity of Lady Macbeth one day by reading aloud the passage that concludes

> . . . I have given suck, and know
> How tender 'tis to love the babe that milks me.
> I would, while it was smiling in my face,
> Have plucked my nipple from his boneless
> gums. . . .

The idea of prim Mr. Fleagle plucking his nipple from boneless gums was too much for the class. We burst into gasps of irrepressible snickering. Mr. Fleagle stopped.

"There is nothing funny, boys, about giving suck to a babe. It is the—the very essence of motherhood, don't you see."

He constantly sprinkled his sentences with "don't you see." It wasn't a question but an exclamation of mild surprise at our ignorance. "Your pronoun needs an antecedent, don't you see," he would say, very primly. "The purpose of the Porter's scene, boys, is to provide comic relief from the horror, don't you see."

Late in the year we tackled the informal essay. "The essay, don't you see, is the . . ." My mind went numb. Of all forms of writing, none seemed so boring as the essay. Naturally we would have to write informal essays. Mr. Fleagle distributed a homework sheet offering us a choice of topics. None was quite so simpleminded as "What I Did on My Summer Vacation," but most seemed to be almost as dull. I took the list home and dawdled until the night before the essay was due. Sprawled on the sofa, I finally faced up to the grim task, took the list out of my notebook, and scanned it. The topic on which my eye stopped was "The Art of Eating Spaghetti."

This title produced an extraordinary sequence of mental images. Surging up out of the depths of memory came a vivid recollection of a night in Belleville when all of us were seated around the supper table—Uncle Allen, my mother, Uncle Charlie, Doris, Uncle Hal—and Aunt Pat served spaghetti for supper. Spaghetti was an exotic treat in those days. Neither Doris nor I had ever eaten spaghetti, and none of the adults had enough experience to be good at it. All the good humor of Uncle Allen's house reawoke in my mind as I recalled the laughing arguments we had that night about the socially respectable method for moving spaghetti from plate to mouth.

Suddenly I wanted to write about that, about the warmth and good feeling of it, but I wanted to put it down simply for my own joy, not for Mr. Fleagle. It was a moment I wanted to recapture and hold for myself. I wanted to relive the pleasure of an evening at New Street. To write it as I wanted, however, would violate all the rules of formal composition I'd learned in school, and Mr. Fleagle would surely give it a failing grade. Never mind. I would write something else for Mr. Fleagle after I had written this thing for myself.

When I finished it the night was half gone and there was no time left to compose a proper, respectable essay for Mr. Fleagle. There was no choice next morning but to turn in my private reminiscence of Belleville. Two days passed before Mr. Fleagle returned the graded papers, and he returned everyone's but mine. I was bracing myself for a command to report to Mr. Fleagle immediately after school for discipline when I saw him lift my paper from his desk and rap for the class's attention.

"Now, boys," he said, "I want to read you an essay. This is titled 'The Art of Eating Spaghetti.'"

And he started to read. My words! He was reading *my words* out loud to the entire class. What's more, the entire class was listening. Listening attentively. Then somebody laughed, then the entire class was laughing, and not in contempt and ridicule, but with openhearted enjoyment. Even Mr. Fleagle stopped two or three times to repress a small prim smile.

I did my best to avoid showing pleasure, but what I was feeling was pure ecstasy at this startling demonstration that my words had the power to make people laugh. In the eleventh grade, at the eleventh hour as it were, I had discovered a calling. It was the happiest moment of my entire school career. When Mr. Fleagle finished he put the final seal on my happiness by saying, "Now that, boys, is an essay, don't you see. It's—don't you see—it's of the very essence of the essay, don't you see. Congratulations, Mr. Baker."

For the first time, light shone on a possibility. It wasn't a very heartening possibility, to be sure. Writing couldn't lead to a job after high school, and it was hardly honest work, but Mr. Fleagle had opened a door for me. After that I ranked Mr. Fleagle among the finest teachers in the school.

My mother was almost as delighted as I when I showed her Mr. Fleagle's A-Plus and described my triumph. Hadn't she always said I had a talent for writing? "Now if you work hard at it, Buddy, you can make something of yourself."

I didn't see how. As the final year of high school neared its end and it began to seem that even the grocery business was beyond me, my mother was also becoming worried.

She'd hoped for years that something would come along to enable me to go to college. All those years she had kept the door open on the possibility that she might turn me into a man of letters. When I was in eighth grade she'd spent precious pennies to subscribe to mail-order bargains in the classics. "World's Greatest Literature," retailing at 39 cents a volume, came in the mail every month, books that stunned me with boredom. *The Last of the Mohicans, Ben Hur, Westward Ho, Vanity Fair, Ivanhoe.* Unread, her attempts to cultivate my literary tastes gathered dust under my bed, but it comforted her to know I had them at my fingertips.

She also subscribed on my behalf to the *Atlantic Monthly* and *Harper's.* "The best magazines in America," she said. "That's where you'll find real writers." The best magazines in America also piled up unread and unreadable in my bedroom. I seemed cut out to serve neither literature nor its bastard offspring, journalism, until my great coup in Mr. Fleagle's English class. Then her hopes revived.

"If only something would come along so you could go to college . . ." became, "For somebody with grades as good as yours, Buddy, there must be some way of getting into college."

Delicately, she spoke to Herb. She could push and haul Herb on matters of household management, but she could scarcely ask him to finance college for me. Grand though his income seemed after her years of poverty, it wasn't big enough to put a boy through college without great sacrifice.

There was also a question of taste. I'd done nothing to endear myself to Herb, and she knew it. What's more, with his few years of elementary school education, Herb would have been flabbergasted by the suggestion that a healthy young man should idle away four years in college at vast expense instead of making his own way in the world as he had done.

Still, my mother did speak to Herb, and Herb listened sympathetically. She told me about it next day. "Herb says he thinks he can get you a job as a brakeman on the B&O," she reported.

"Well," I said, "railroad men make good pay."

"Maybe something will come along before school's out," she said.

The idea of becoming a railroad brakeman entertained me for a while that winter. Any job prospect would have interested me then. I was becoming embarrassed about being one of the few boys in the class with no plan for the future. The editors of the high-school yearbook circulated a questionnaire among members of the senior class asking each student to reveal his career ambition. I could hardly put down "To be a writer." That would have made me look silly. Boys of the Depression generation were expected to have their hearts set on money-making work. To reply "Ambition: None" was unthinkable. You were supposed to have had your eye on a high goal from the day you left knee pants. Boys who hadn't yet decided on a specific career usually replied that their ambition was "to be a success." That was all right. The Depression had made materialists of us all; almost everybody wanted "to be a success."

I studied the yearbook questionnaire with deepening despair. I wanted the yearbook to record for posterity that I had once had flaming ambition, but I could think of nothing very exciting. Finally I turned to my friend Bob Eckert in the desk behind me.

"What are you putting down for ambition?" I asked.

"Foreign correspondent," Eckert said.

I loved it. It sounded dashing, thrilling. Unfortunately, it was so different, so exciting an "ambition," that I couldn't copy Eckert without looking like a cheat. And so, turning my mind to journalism, I ticked off other glamorous newspaper jobs and after a moment's reflection wrote down, "To be a newspaper columnist."

In fact I hadn't the least interest in journalism and no ambition whatever to be a newspaper columnist. Though City College published an excellent weekly newspaper, during my four years there I was never interested enough to apply for a job, never knew where its office was located, and never cared enough to find out.

Having solved the problem of finding an "ambition" elegant enough for the yearbook, I returned to reality. Was I really sharp enough to make it in the retail grocery business? Should I become a railroad man?

Matters were at this stage in the spring of 1942 when I discovered my great friend and classmate Charlie Sussman filling out a sheaf of forms between classes one day. Sussman was a prodigious bookworm and lover of education. I admired him greatly for the wide range of his knowledge, which far exceeded mine. He understood the distinction between fascism and communism, subjects on which I was utterly ignorant. He was interested in politics and foreign policy, subjects that bored me. He listened to classical music, to which I was completely deaf. He planned to become a teacher and had the instinct for it. It bothered him that there were such great gaps in my education. Like my mother, Sussman wanted to improve me. He tried to awaken me to the beauties of music. "Start with Tchaikovsky," he pleaded. "Tchaikovsky is easy. Everybody likes Tchaikovsky. Then you'll discover the beauty of Beethoven and Mozart."

Now, finding him bent over a strange batch of papers, I asked, "What're you doing, Suss?"

"Filling out college application forms," he said.

"What college are you going to?"

"Johns Hopkins," he said.

I knew that Johns Hopkins was a hospital and produced doctors.

"I didn't know you wanted to be a doctor. I thought you wanted to teach."

"Hopkins isn't just for doctors," he said.

"No kidding."

"It's a regular college too," he said. "What college are you going to?"

"I'm not going to college."

Sussman was shocked. Dropping his pen, he glared at me in amazement. "Not going to college?" He said it in outrage. He refused to tolerate this offense to education. "You've got to go to college," he said. "Get some admission forms—they've got them downstairs at the office—and we'll go to Hopkins together."

That would be great, I said, but my family couldn't afford it.

"Apply for a scholarship," he commanded.

"What's that?"

Sussman explained. I was astonished. It seemed that this college, of whose existence I had just learned, was willing to accept a limited number of students absolutely free if they could do well on a competitive examination. Sussman himself intended to take the test in hope of reducing the cost to his parents.

"I'll get you a set of application forms," he said, and he did. He was determined that education would not lose me without a struggle.

My mother was as surprised as I'd been. Just when she had begun to lose faith that something would come along, providence had assumed the shape of Charlie Sussman and smiled upon us. The day of the examination she stopped me as I was going out the door and kissed me.

"I've been praying for you every night," she said. "You'll do great."

She'd been doing more than praying. For three weeks she'd worked with me every night on a home refresher course in mathematics, my weakest subject. Night after night she held the math books and conducted quizzes on geometry and algebra, laboriously checking my solutions against those in the back of the books and, when I erred, struggling along with me to discover where I'd gone wrong. Afterwards, when we were both worn out, she went to bed and prayed. She believed in prayer, in the Lord's intercession, but not in the Lord's willingness to do it all. She and I together had to help. The Lord helped those who helped themselves.

The examination was held on a Saturday in May. I hadn't been to Johns Hopkins before, so I gave myself an extra hour against the possibility of getting lost on the streetcar trip to North Baltimore. My mother had written the directions and put them in my pocket, just in case, but the trip went smoothly, and when I reached the campus I was directed to a huge lecture hall reeking of chemicals. I was dismayed to find the hall filled with boys, each of whom probably wanted one of the few available scholarships as desperately as I did.

Unlike my mother, I had no faith in prayer. From early

childhood I had thought of God as a cosmic trick player. Though I'd never told this to my mother and went to church regularly to please her, I'd grown up a fatalist with little faith. Now, though, as I counted the boys in the room and realized the odds against me, I decided it was foolish to leave even the remotest possibility untouched. Closing my eyes, I silently uttered the Lord's Prayer in my head and, to leave no base untouched, followed it with the only other prayer I knew, the one my mother had taught me years ago when putting me to bed in Morrisonville. And so, as the examination papers were being distributed, I sat at my desk silently repeating, "Now I lay me down to sleep, I pray the Lord my soul to keep . . ."

At the end I improvised a single line of my own and prayed, "Dear God, help me with this test." It lasted four hours.

My mother was waiting on the porch when I came back down Marydell Road that afternoon. "How'd it go, Buddy?"

"Don't know," I said, which I didn't.

Two weeks crept slowly past and May neared its end. I had only three weeks left of high school when I arrived home one afternoon to find my mother sitting expressionless in the glider on the front porch. "You got a letter from Hopkins today," she said. "It's in on the table."

"Did you open it?"

"I'm not in the habit of opening other people's mail," she said. "You open it and tell me what it says."

We went inside together. The envelope was there on the table. It was a very small envelope. Very small. Hopkins had obviously decided I was not worth wasting much stationery on. Picking it up, I saw that it was also very thin. The message was obviously short and probably not sweet if it could be conveyed in such flimsy form. I ripped the end off the envelope, slid out a piece of note-sized paper, and unfolded it. I saw it was a form letter on which someone had typed a few words in the blank spaces. I read it to myself.

"Well, what does it say?" my mother asked.

I read it aloud to her:

> Sir: I am pleased to inform you that you have been awarded a Hopkins Scholarship for two terms of the academic year 1942-43. This award will entitle you to remission of tuition fees for this period. Please let me know at once if you will accept this award.
>
> Yours very truly,
> Isaiah Bowman
> President

"Let me read it," my mother said. She did, and she smiled, and she read it again; then she said, "Herb is going to be proud of you, Buddy."

"What about you?" I asked.

"Well, I always knew you could do it," she said heading for the kitchen. "I think I'll make us some iced tea."

She had to do something ordinary, I suppose, or risk fainting with delight. We had helped ourselves, the Lord had helped us in return, and one of her wildest dreams had come true. Something had come along.

from

ARABY

JAMES JOYCE

Unlike Russell Baker, the hero of James Joyce's story
"Araby" is full of dreams, willowy dreams of a
beautiful young girl and the exotic wonders of all that
she means to him. Seeing the gulf between dreams
and reality that he eventually sees is a defining aspect
of coming of age. Getting across is another story.

North Richmond Street, being blind, was a quiet street except at the hour when the Christian Brothers' School set the boys free. An uninhabited house of two storeys stood at the blind end, detached from its neighbours in a square ground. The other houses of the street, conscious of decent lives within them, gazed at one another with brown imperturbable faces.

The former tenant of our house, a priest, had died in the back drawing-room. Air, musty from having been long enclosed, hung in all the rooms, and the waste room behind the kitchen was littered with old useless papers. Among these I found a few paper-covered books, the pages of which were curled and damp: *The Abbot,* by Walter Scott, *The Devout Communicant* and *The Memoirs of Vidocq.* I liked the last best because its leaves were yellow. The wild garden behind the house contained a central apple-tree and a few straggling bushes under one of which I found the late tenant's rusty bicycle-pump. He had been a very charitable priest; in his will he had left all his money to institutions and the furniture of his house to his sister.

When the short days of winter came dusk fell before we had well eaten our dinners. When we met in the street the houses had grown sombre. The space of sky above us was the colour of ever-changing violet and towards it the lamps of the street lifted their feeble lanterns. The cold air stung us and we played till our bodies glowed. Our shouts echoed in the silent street. The career of our play brought us through the dark muddy lanes behind the houses where we ran the gantlet of the rough tribes from the cottages, to the back doors of the dark dripping gardens where odours arose from the ashpits, to the dark odorous stables where a coachman smoothed and combed the horse or shook music from the buckled harness. When we returned to the street light from the kitchen windows had filled the areas. If my uncle was seen turning the corner we hid in the shadow until we had seen him safely housed. Or if Mangan's sister came out on the doorstep to call her brother in to his tea we watched her from our shadow peer up and down the street. We waited to see whether she would remain or go in and, if she remained, we left our shadow and walked up to Mangan's steps resignedly. She was waiting for us, her figure defined by the light from the half-opened door. Her brother always teased her before he obeyed and I stood by the railings looking at her. Her dress swung as she moved her body and the soft rope of her hair tossed from side to side.

Every morning I lay on the floor in the front parlour watching her door. The blind was pulled down to within an inch of the sash so that I could not be seen. When she came out on the doorstep my heart leaped. I ran to the hall, seized my books and followed her. I kept her brown figure always in my eye and, when we came near the point at which our ways diverged, I quickened my pace and passed her. This happened morning after morning. I had never spoken to her, except for a few casual words, and yet her name was like a summons to all my foolish blood.

Her image accompanied me even in places the most hostile to romance. On Saturday evenings when my aunt went marketing I had to go to carry some of the parcels. We walked through the flaring streets, jostled by drunken men and bargaining women, amid the curses of labourers, the shrill litanies of shop-boys who stood on guard by the barrels of pigs' cheeks, the nasal chanting of street-singers, who sang a *come-all-you* about O'Donovan Rossa, or a ballad about the troubles in our native land. These noises converged in a single sensation of life for me: I imagined that I bore my chalice safely through a throng of foes. Her name sprang to my lips at moments in strange prayers and praises which I myself did not understand. My eyes were often full of tears (I could not tell why) and at times a flood from my heart seemed to pour itself out into my bosom. I thought little of the future. I did not know whether I would ever speak to her or not or, if I spoke to her, how I could tell her of my confused adoration. But my body was like a harp and her words and gestures were like fingers running upon the wires.

One evening I went into the back drawing-room in which the priest had died. It was a dark rainy evening and there was no sound in the house. Through one of the broken panes I heard the rain impinge upon the earth, the fine incessant needles of water playing in the sodden beds. Some distant lamp or lighted window gleamed below me. I was thankful that I could see so little. All my senses seemed to desire to veil themselves and, feeling that I was about to slip from them, I pressed the palms of my hands together until they trembled, murmuring: *O love! O love!* many times.

At last she spoke to me. When she addressed the first words to me I was so confused that I did not know what to answer. She asked me was I going to *Araby*. I forget whether I answered yes or no. It would be a splendid bazaar, she said; she would love to go.

—And why can't you? I asked.

While she spoke she turned a silver bracelet round and round her wrist. She could not go, she said, because there would be a retreat that week in her convent. Her brother and two other boys were fighting for their caps and I was alone at the railings. She held one of the spikes, bowing her head towards me. The light from the lamp opposite our door caught the white curve of her neck, lit up her hair that rested there and, falling, lit up the hand upon the railing. It fell over one side of her dress and caught the white border of a petticoat, just visible as she stood at ease.

—It's well for you, she said.

—If I go, I said, I will bring you something.

What innumerable follies laid waste my waking and

sleeping thoughts after that evening! I wished to annihilate the tedious intervening days. I chafed against the work of school. At night in my bedroom and by day in the classroom her image came between me and the page I strove to read. The syllables of the word *Araby* were called to me through the silence in which my soul luxuriated and cast an Eastern enchantment over me. I asked for leave to go to the bazaar Saturday night. My aunt was surprised and hoped it was not some Freemason affair. I answered few questions in class. I watched my master's face pass from amiability to sternness; he hoped I was not beginning to idle. I could not call my wandering thoughts together. I had hardly any patience with the serious work of life which, now that it stood between me and my desire, seemed to me child's play, ugly monotonous child's play.

On Saturday morning I reminded my uncle that I wished to go to the bazaar in the evening. He was fussing at the hall-stand, looking for the hat-brush, and answered me curtly:

—Yes, boy, I know.

As he was in the hall I could not go into the front parlour and lie at the window. I left the house in bad humour and walked slowly towards the school. The air was pitilessly raw and already my heart misgave me.

When I came home to dinner my uncle had not yet been home. Still it was early. I sat staring at the clock for some time and, when its ticking began to irritate me, I left the room. I mounted the staircase and gained the upper part of the house. The high cold empty gloomy rooms liberated me and I went from room to room singing. From the front window I saw my companions playing below in the street. Their cries reached me weakened and indistinct and, leaning my forehead against the cool glass, I looked over at the dark house where she lived. I may have stood there for an hour, seeing nothing but the brown-clad figure cast by my imagination, touched discreetly by the lamplight at the curved neck, at the hand upon the railings and at the border below the dress.

When I came downstairs again I found Mrs Mercer sitting at the fire. She was an old garrulous woman, a pawnbroker's widow, who collected used stamps for some pious purpose. I had to endure the gossip of the tea-table. The meal was prolonged beyond an hour and still my uncle did not come. Mrs Mercer stood up to go: she was sorry she couldn't wait any longer, but it was after eight o'clock and she did not like to be out late, as the night air was bad for her. When she had gone I began to walk up and down the room, clenching my fists. My aunt said:

—I'm afraid you may put off your bazaar for this night of Our Lord.

At nine o'clock I heard my uncle's latchkey in the halldoor. I heard him talking to himself and heard the hallstand rocking when it had received the weight of his overcoat. I could interpret these signs. When he was midway through his dinner I asked him to give me the money to go to the bazaar. He had forgotten.

—The people are in bed and after their first sleep now, he said.

I did not smile. My aunt said to him energetically:

—Can't you give him the money and let him go? You've kept him late enough as it is.

My uncle said he was very sorry he had forgotten. He said he believed in the old saying: *All work and no play makes Jack a dull boy.* He asked me where I was going and, when I had told him a second time he asked me did I know *The Arab's Farewell to his Steed.* When I left the kitchen he was about to recite the opening lines of the piece to my aunt.

I held a florin tightly in my hand as I strode down Buckingham Street towards the station. The sight of the streets thronged with buyers and glaring with gas recalled to me the purpose of my journey. I took my seat in a third-class carriage of a deserted train. After an intolerable delay the train moved out of the station slowly. It crept onward among ruinous houses and over the twinkling river. At Westland Row Station a crowd of people pressed to the carriage doors; but the porters moved them back, saying that it was a special train for the bazaar. I remained alone in the bare carriage. In a few minutes the train drew up beside an improvised wooden platform. I passed out on to the road and saw by the lighted dial of a clock that it was ten minutes to ten. In front of me was a large building which displayed the magical name.

I could not find any sixpenny entrance and, fearing that the bazaar would be closed, I passed in quickly through a turnstile, handing a shilling to a weary-looking man. I found myself in a big hall girdled at half its height by a gallery. Nearly all the stalls were closed and the greater part of the hall was in darkness. I recognised a silence like that which pervades a church after a service. I walked into the centre of the bazaar timidly. A few people were gathered about the stalls which were still open. Before a curtain, over which the words *Café Chantant* were written in coloured lamps, two men were counting money on a salver. I listened to the fall of the coins.

Remembering with difficulty why I had come I went over to one of the stalls and examined porcelain vases and flowered tea-sets. At the door of the stall a young lady was talking and laughing with two young gentlemen. I remarked their English accents and listened vaguely to their conversation.

—O, I never said such a thing!

—O, but you did!

—O, but I didn't!

—Didn't she say that?

—Yes. I heard her.

—O, there's a . . . fib!

f r o m A R A B Y

Observing me the young lady came over and asked me did I wish to buy anything. The tone of her voice was not encouraging; she seemed to have spoken to me out of a sense of duty. I looked humbly at the great jars that stood like eastern guards at either side of the dark entrance to the stall and murmured:

—No, thank you.

The young lady changed the position of one of the vases and went back to the two young men. They began to talk of the same subject. Once or twice the young lady glanced at me over her shoulder.

I lingered before her stall, though I knew my stay was useless, to make my interest in her wares seem the more real. Then I turned away slowly and walked down the middle of the bazaar. I allowed the two pennies to fall against the sixpence in my pocket. I heard a voice call from one end of the gallery that the light was out. The upper part of the hall was now completely dark.

Gazing up into the darkness I saw myself as a creature driven and derided by vanity; and my eyes burned with anguish and anger.

from

A TREE GROWS
IN BROOKLYN

BETTY SMITH

Coming of age has some very physical manifestations,
particularly the one that the heroine of Betty Smith's
novel encounters in this selection. While the change
in her body is immense, it is the change in how she
now thinks because of it that affects her more.

"Today, I am a woman," wrote Francie in her diary in the summer when she was thirteen. She looked at the sentence and absently scratched a mosquito bite on her bare leg. She looked down on her long thin and as yet formless legs. She crossed out the sentence and started over. "Soon, I shall become a woman." She looked down on her chest which was as flat as a washboard and ripped the page out of the book. She started fresh on a new page.

"Intolerance," she wrote, pressing down hard on the pencil, "is a thing that causes war, pogroms, crucifixions, lynchings, and makes people cruel to little children and to each other. It is responsible for most of the viciousness, violence, terror and heart and soul breaking of the world."

She read the words over aloud. They sounded like words that came in a can; the freshness was cooked out of them. She closed the book and put it away.

That summer Saturday was a day that should have gone down in her diary as one of the happiest days of her life. She saw her name in print for the first time. The school got out a magazine at the end of the year in which the best story written in composition class from each grade was published. Francie's composition called "Winter Time" had been chosen as the best of the seventh grade work. The magazine cost a dime and Francie had had to wait until Saturday to get it. School closed for the summer the day before and Francie worried that she wouldn't get the magazine. But Mr. Jenson said he'd be working around on Saturday and if she brought the dime over, he'd give her a copy.

Now in the early afternoon, she stood in front of her door with the magazine opened to the page of her story. She hoped someone would come along to whom she could show it.

She had shown it to mama at lunch time but mama had to get back to work and didn't have time to read it. At least five times during lunch, Francie mentioned that she had a story published. At last mama said,

"Yes, yes. I know. I saw it all coming. There'll be more stories printed and you'll get used to it. Now don't let it go to your head. There are dishes to be washed."

Papa was at Union Headquarters. He wouldn't see the story till Sunday but Francie knew he'd be pleased. So she stood on the street with her glory tucked under her arm. She couldn't let the magazine out of her hands even for a moment. From time to time she'd glance at her name in print and the excitement about it never grew less.

She saw a girl named Joanna come out of her house a few doors away. Joanna was taking her baby out for an airing in its carriage. A gasp came up from some housewives who had stopped to gossip on the sidewalk while going to and fro about their shopping. You see, Joanna was not married. She was a girl who had gotten into trouble. Her baby was illegitimate—bastard was the word they used in the neighborhood—and these good women felt that Joanna had no right to act like a proud mother and bring her baby out into the light of day. They felt that she should have kept it hidden in some dark place.

Francie was curious about Joanna and the baby. She had heard mama and papa talking about them. She stared at the baby when the carriage came by. It was a beautiful little thing sitting up happily in its carriage. Maybe Joanna *was* a bad girl but certainly she kept her baby sweeter and daintier than these good women kept theirs. The baby wore a pretty frilled bonnet and a clean white dress and bib. The carriage cover was spotless and showed much loving handiwork in its embroidery.

Joanna worked in a factory while her mother took care of the baby. The mother was too ashamed to take it out so the baby got an airing only on week-ends when Joanna wasn't working.

Yes, Francie decided, it was a beautiful baby. It looked just like Joanna. Francie remembered how papa had described her that day he and mama were talking about her.

"She has skin like a magnolia petal." (Johnny had never seen a magnolia.) "Her hair is as black as a raven's wing." (He had never seen such a bird.) "And her eyes are deep and dark like forest pools." (He had never been in a forest and the only pool he knew was where each man put in a dime and guessed what the Dodgers score would be and whoever guessed right got all the dimes.) But he had described Joanna accurately. She was a beautiful girl.

"That may be," answered Katie. "But what good is her looks? They're a curse to the girl. I heard that her mother was never married but had two children just the same. And now the mother's son is in Sing Sing and her daughter has this baby. There must be bad blood all along the line and no use getting sentimental about it. Of course," she added with a detachment of which she was astonishingly capable at times, "it's none of my business. I don't need to do anything about it one way or the other. I don't need to go out and spit on the girl because she did wrong. Neither do I have to take her in my house and adopt her because she did wrong. She suffered as much pain bringing that child into the world as though she *was* married. If she's a good girl at heart, she'll learn from the pain and the shame and she won't do it again. If she's naturally bad, it won't bother her the way people treat her. So, if I was you, Johnny, I wouldn't feel too sorry for her." Suddenly she turned to Francie and said, "Let Joanna be a lesson to *you*."

On this Saturday afternoon, Francie watched Joanna walk up and down and wondered in what way she was a lesson.

Joanna acted proud about her baby. Was the lesson there? Joanna was only seventeen and friendly and she wanted everybody to be friendly with her. She smiled at the grim good women but the smile went away when she saw that they answered her with frowns. She smiled at the little children playing on the street. Some smiled back. She smiled at Francie. Francie wanted to smile back but didn't. Was the lesson that she mustn't be friendly with girls like Joanna?

The good housewives, their arms filled with bags of vegetables and brown paper parcels of meat, seemed to have little to do that afternoon. They kept gathering into little knots and whispered to each other. The whispering stopped when Joanna came by and started up when she had passed.

Each time Joanna passed, her cheeks got pinker, her head went higher and her skirt flipped behind her more defiantly. She seemed to grow prettier and prouder as she walked. She stopped oftener than needed to adjust the baby's coverlet. She maddened the women by touching the baby's cheek and smiling tenderly at it. How dare she! How dare she, they thought, act as though she had a right to all that?

Many of these good women had children which they brought up by scream and cuff. Many of them hated the husbands who lay by their sides at night. There was no longer high joy for them in the act of love. They endured the lovemaking rigidly, praying all the while that another child would not result. This bitter submissiveness made the man ugly and brutal. To most of them the love act had become a brutality on both sides; the sooner over with, the better. They resented this girl because they felt this had not been so with her and the father of her child.

Joanna recognized their hate but wouldn't cringe before it. She would not give in and take the baby indoors. Something *had* to give. The women broke first. They couldn't endure it any longer. They had to do something about it. The next time Joanna passed, a stringy woman called out:

"Ain't you ashamed of yourself?"

"What for?" Joanna wanted to know.

This infuriated the woman. "What for, she asks," she reported to the other women. "I'll tell you what for. Because you're a disgrace and a bum. You got no right to parade the streets with your bastard where innocent children can see you."

"I guess this is a free country," said Joanna.

"Not free for the likes of you. Get off the street, get off the street."

"Try and make me!"

"Get off the street, you whore," ordered the stringy woman.

The girl's voice trembled when she answered. "Be careful what you're saying."

"We don't have to be careful what we say to no street walker," chipped in another woman.

A man passing by stopped a moment to take it in. He touched Joanna's arm. "Look, Sister, why don't you go home till these battle-axes cool off? You can't win with them."

Joanna jerked her arm away. "You mind your own business!"

"I meant it in the right way, Sister. Sorry." He walked on.

"Why don't you go with him," taunted the stringy woman. "He might be good for a quarter." The others laughed.

"You're all jealous," said Joanna evenly.

"She says we're jealous," reported the interlocutor. "Jealous of what, you?" (She said "you" as though it were the girl's name.)

"Jealous that men like me. That's what. Lucky you're married already," she told the stringy one. "You'd never get a man otherwise. I bet your husband spits on you—afterwards. I bet that's just what he does."

"Bitch! You bitch!" screamed the stringy one hysterically. Then, acting on an instinct which was strong even in Christ's day, she picked a stone out of the gutter and threw it at Joanna.

It was the signal for the other women to start throwing stones. One, droller than the rest, threw a ball of horse manure. Some of the stones hit Joanna but a sharp pointed one missed and struck the baby's forehead. Immediately, a thin clear trickle of blood ran down the baby's face and spotted its clean bib. The baby whimpered and held out its arms for its mother to pick it up.

A few women, poised to throw the next stones, dropped them quietly back into the gutter. The baiting was all over. Suddenly the women were ashamed. They had not wanted to hurt the baby. They only wanted to drive Joanna off the street. They dispersed and went home quietly. Some children who had been standing around listening, resumed their play.

Joanna, crying now, lifted the baby from the carriage. The baby continued to whimper quietly as though it had no right to cry out loud. Joanna pressed her cheek to her baby's face and her tears mixed with its blood. The women won. Joanna carried her baby into the house not caring that the carriage stood in the middle of the sidewalk.

And Francie had seen it all; had seen it all. She had heard every word. She remembered how Joanna had smiled at her and how she had turned her head away without smiling back. Why hadn't she smiled back? Why hadn't she smiled back? Now she would suffer—she would suffer all the rest of her life every time that she remembered that she had not smiled back.

Some small boys started to play tag around the empty carriage, holding on to its sides and pulling it way over while being chased. Francie scattered them and wheeled the carriage over to Joanna's door and put the brake on. There was an unwritten law that nothing was to be molested that stood outside the door where it belonged.

She was still holding the magazine with her story in it. She stood next to the braked carriage and looked at her name once more. "Winter Time, by Frances Nolan." She wanted to do something, sacrifice something to pay for not having smiled at Joanna. She thought of her story, she was so proud of it; so eager to show papa and Aunt Evy and Sissy. She wanted to keep it always to look at and to get that nice warm feeling when she looked at it. If she gave it away, there was no means by which she could get another copy. She slipped the magazine under the baby's pillow. She left it open at the page of her story.

She saw some tiny drops of blood on the baby's snowy pillow. Again she saw the baby; the thin trickle of blood on its face; the way it held out its arms to be taken up. A wave of hurt broke over Francie and left her weak when it passed. Another wave came, broke and receded. She found her way down to the cellar of her house and sat in the darkest corner on a heap of burlap sacks and waited while the hurt waves swept over her. As each wave spent itself and a new one gathered, she trembled. Tensely she sat there waiting for them to stop. If they didn't stop, she'd have to die—she'd have to die.

After awhile they came fainter and there was a longer time between each one. She began to think. She was now getting her lesson from Joanna but it was not the kind of lesson her mother meant.

She remembered Joanna. Often at night on her way

home from the library, she had passed Joanna's house and seen her and the boy standing close together in the narrow vestibule. She had seen the boy stroke Joanna's pretty hair tenderly; had seen how Joanna put up her hand to touch his cheek. And Joanna's face looked peaceful and dreamy in the light from the street lamp. Out of that beginning, then, had come the shame and the baby. Why? Why? The beginning had seemed so tender and so right. Why?

She knew that one of the women stone-throwers had had a baby only three months after her marriage. Francie had been one of the children standing at the curb watching the party leave for the church. She saw the bulge of pregnancy under the virginal veil of the bride as she stepped into the hired carriage. She saw the hand of the father closed tight on the bridegroom's arm. The groom had black shadows under his eyes and looked very sad.

Joanna had no father, no men kin. There was no one to hold her boy's arm tight on the way to the altar. That was Joanna's crime, decided Francie—not that she had been bad, but that she had not been smart enough to get the boy to the church.

Francie had no way of knowing the whole story. As a matter of fact, the boy loved Joanna and was willing to marry her after—as the saying goes—he had gotten her into trouble. The boy had a family—a mother and three sisters. He told them he wanted to marry Joanna and they talked him out of it.

Don't be a fool, they told him. She's no good. Her whole family's no good. Besides, how do you know you're the one? If she had you she had others. Oh, women are tricky. We know. We are women. You are good and tender-hearted. You take her word for it that you are the man. She lies. Don't be tricked my son, don't be tricked, our brother. If you must marry, marry a good girl, one who won't sleep with you without the priest saying the words that make it right. If you marry this girl, you are no longer my son; you are no longer our brother. You'll never be sure whether the child is yours. You will worry while you are at your work. You'll wonder who slips into your bed beside her after you have left in the morning. Oh yes, my son, our brother, that is how women do. *We* know. *We* are women. *We* know how they do.

The boy had let himself be persuaded. His women folk gave him money and he got a room and a new job over in Jersey. They wouldn't tell Joanna where he was. He never saw her again. Joanna wasn't married. Joanna had the baby.

The waves had almost stopped passing over Francie when she discovered to her fright that something was wrong with her. She pressed her hand over her heart trying to feel a jagged edge under the flesh. She had heard papa sing so many songs about the heart; the heart that was breaking— was aching—was dancing—was heavy laden—that leaped for joy—that was heavy in sorrow—that turned over—that stood still. She really believed that the heart actually did those things. She was terrified thinking her heart had broken inside her over Joanna's baby and that the blood was now leaving her heart and flowing from her body.

She went upstairs to the flat and looked into the mirror. Her eyes had dark shadows beneath them and her head was aching. She lay on the old leather couch in the kitchen and waited for mama to come home.

She told mama what had happened to her in the cellar. She said nothing about Joanna. Katie sighed and said, "So soon? You're just thirteen. I didn't think it would come for another year yet. I was fifteen."

"Then . . . then . . . this is all right what's happening?"

"It's a natural thing that comes to all women."

"I'm not a woman."

"It means you're changing from a girl into a woman."

"Do you think it will go away?"

"In a few days. But it will come back again in a month."

"For how long?"

"For a long time. Until you are forty or even fifty." She mused awhile. "My mother was fifty when I was born."

"Oh, it has something to do with having babies."

"Yes. Remember always to be a good girl because you can have a baby now." Joanna and her baby flashed through Francie's mind. "You mustn't let the boys kiss you," said mama.

"Is that how you get a baby?"

"No. But what makes you get a baby often starts with a kiss." She added, "Remember Joanna."

Now Katie didn't know about the street scene. Joanna happened to pop into her mind. But Francie thought she had wonderful powers of insight. She looked at mama with new respect.

Remember Joanna. Remember Joanna. Francie could never forget her. From that time on, remembering the stoning women, she hated women. She feared them for their devious ways, she mistrusted their instincts. She began to hate them for this disloyalty and their cruelty to each other. Of all the stone-throwers, not one had dared to speak a word for the girl for fear that she would be tarred with Joanna's brush. The passing man had been the only one who spoke with kindness in his voice.

Most women had the one thing in common: they had great pain when they gave birth to their children. This should make a bond that held them all together; it should make them love and protect each other against the man-world. But it was not so. It seemed like their great birth pains shrank their hearts and their souls. They stuck together for only one thing: to trample on some other woman . . . whether it was by throwing stones or by mean gossip. It was the only kind of loyalty they seemed to have.

Men were different. They might hate each other but they stuck together against the world and against any woman who would ensnare one of them.

Francie opened the copybook which she used for a diary. She skipped a line under the paragraph that she had written about intolerance and wrote:

"As long as I live, I will never have a woman for a friend. I will never trust any woman again, except maybe mama and sometimes Aunt Evy and Aunt Sissy."

from

TRAIN WHISTLE GUITAR

ALBERT MURRAY

The hero of Albert Murray's novel may lose his
virginity at an early age, but it is a long time and
many girls before he learns the truth about that
event. Only then does he truly come of age.

Deljean McCray, who was as cinnamon-bark brown as was the cinnamon-brown bark she was forever chewing and smelling like, and who is always the girl I remember when I remember dog fennels and dog fennel meadows, was that much older and that much taller than I was at that time, and she was also two grades ahead of me in school then. So when she finally said what I had been waiting and wishing all day for her to say about me that Wednesday while Miss Tee was downtown shopping, I crossed my fingers.

Then I said what I said. I said Cute is what some folks say about monkeys and puppies, and I held my breath and waited for her to say That's all right about some old monkeys and puppies, ain't nobody talking about no monkeys and puppies I'm talking about you, and she did and poked out her mouth, and she was also trying to roll her eyes. But she couldn't look scornful because she couldn't keep her eyes from twinkling at the same time. Then she started grinning to herself but as if for both of us.

So I said What's so funny girl, but only to be saying something. Because I knew we were thinking about the same thing, which was that Miss Tee, who was the only one who knew we were there by ourselves, was not due back until half-past three. Mama knew where I was (as she usually did, or so she thought) and she knew who else was there because everybody knew where Deljean McCray, who was Miss Tee's husband's niece, was staying that year. But nobody knew that Miss Tee herself was not only not there but was all the way downtown at Askins Marine. Except us. To whom, by the way, her only word had been: If anybody come tell them I say I'll be back directly.

You, Deljean McCray said still pretending to pout, that's what. And I held my fingers crossed but I could hardly keep myself from grinning for another reason.

Because I was thinking about Little Buddy and old Gander Gallagher who were shrimping and crabbing together somewhere near or under One Mile Bridge that day and who thought I was not supposed to go anywhere beyond the chinaberry yard because I was being punished—and who could not possibly know that I was only now on the verge of getting my very first chance to do what they had never let me deny I had been doing all along.

We were in that part of the house because that was where we had brought the clothesbasket, and she was standing at the long table because that was where she was separating what she was supposed to press from all the starched shirts and dresses that had to be sprinkled to be ironed by Miss Tee herself. I was sitting straddling the turned-around cane-bottom chair by the window, and outside there was the castor bean plant. Then there was the chicken yard, and beyond that was the empty clothesline; and you could also see across the garden fence and pass the live oak tree to the meadow and the tank yard.

I kept my fingers crossed because that was the way I already was about almost everything even then. Because by that time I knew better than to take anything for granted even when it was something you had not only been promised but had also been reassured about. The best way was to wait and see, as you had long since learned to do at santaclaustime and for birthday presents. Anyway I was not about to make any country breaks that day. Not with Deljean McCray.

She said she bet me that was what I did like, and I said I bet I didn't either, and she said I bet you do too. I bet you that's exactly what you do like, a puppy dog a littleold hassle mouth frisky tail daddy fyce puppy dog. And she kept on grinning her cinnamon bark grin to herself looking at me sideways. So I frowned and looked out through the window and across the dog fennel meadow to the pine ridge sky above Chickasabogue Creek and Hog Bayou Swamp, but I was almost grinning to myself in spite of myself then because she was the one who had said it first. So all I said was How come you say that, and she said Because, and I said Because what, girl, and she said don't be calling her no girl.

Little old mister boy, she said.

Well, *miss* girl then, I said. Because what miss girl?

Because you don't even know what I'm talking about, that's what, she said, and I said That's what you say.

Because I did know. Because I already knew about all of that even before that time playing house with Charlene Wingate when I was not only caught and not only spanked and chastised but also threatened with the booger man who would catch you and cut off your thing with his butcher knife.

That's what you say, I said, but that don't make it so, and that was when she said Well I bet you, and I said Bet me what, and she said You guess what since you know so much about it, and I said okay, and I almost uncrossed my fingers. But I didn't. Because I could hardly wait, but I knew I had to. So all I did was get up from the chair with my fingers crossed in my left pocket.

I was standing that close to her and the Vaseline sheen of her cinnamon scented braids then, and she said: You know something you a mannish little old boy, Scooter. You just as mannish as you can be. Boy, who you call yourself getting mannish with? Boy, what you think you trying to do? Boy you better let your pants alone. Boy, who told you to come trying to start something like that? Ohh Scooter.

She moved back to the wall then and said Ohh Scooter look at you. Look at yours. Look at you already swelling up like that. Did a wasp sting you or something. Oh Scooter you mannish rascal you. But see there you ain't got no hairs like me yet. Just like I thought. See there. Look at me.

Look at my titties like a big girl, she said, smelling almost as much like sardines as cinnamon. Look at my hairs like a wasp nest. And she bent her knees with her back against the wall and put her hands inside her thighs around her dog fennel meadow and her sardine slit. See there. I'm already a big girl little old mannish boy. I'm already big enough to get knocked up. Because a girl grown enough to have a baby just as soon as she old enough to start ministrating. If I was to do it with a sure enough man and he was to shoot off and big me he got to marry me unless he want to go to jail.

That was also when she said what she also said about boys being different. Boys can get stunted: Little old mannish tail boys start messing around with too many big girls and grown women before you man enough and you know what? You subject to hurt yourself and come up stunted for the rest of your life. That's what they say happened to Billy Goat. They say somebody got a hold to him and turned him every way but loose and now his too big for the rest of his body, and that's how come he have them falling out spells gagging and foaming at the mouth. Some old hard woman bring your nature down too soon and that's when it go to your head and you start craving and playing with yourself and skeeting all the time and goodbye, sonny boy.

That's all right about Goat Bascomb, I said thinking also of Knot Newberry the hunchback who went around whispering and giggling to himself. That's Goat. That ain't got nothing to do with me.

Because if I was going to be stunted I would have already

been stunted a long time ago, I said and she said: Who you think you trying to fool, Scooter? Who you think this is you talking to? Who you trying to say you been doing something like that with little old mannish pisstail boy?

Girl you know good and well ain't nobody supposed to tell you who nobody was, I said.

And I bet you I know why too, she said. Because it ain't nobody that's why. Because I sure know one thing. It wasn't nobody big as me. And little old pisstail gals don't count. Because I bet you I already know who it was anyhow. Because it ain't nobody but little old Charlene Wingate with her little old half stuck-up frizzly-headed self, and she sure don't count because she ain't got no more than some little old pimples on her little flat bosom and I bet you anything she ain't got no hairs yet.

That's all right about who it was, I said and I was also about to say that's all right about big girls and grown women and all that too, but that was when I realized that she was standing there grinning at me sideways because she was probably waiting for me to be the one to make the next move. So I said something else.

You said you bet me Deljean, I said. You the one said you bet me.

Well come on then little old mannish boy, she said. Since you think you already such a mister big man. What you standing there sticking out like that for?

• • •

That was that first time with Deljean McCray (on the floor under the tent top of the table with my fingers crossed all the while) and she kept saying What you doing boy? Boy what you think you doing you little fresh tail rascal. Boy, Scooter I declare. Boy, Scooter here you doing something like this. Oh see there what you doing? Now sure enough now Scooter now boy now you know good and well we not supposed to be doing nothing like this.

Then she said Now that's enough now Scooter so you stop now and I mean it too now Scooter. Get up off of me boy. You get your fresh-ass self down off me. Then we were standing up again and she said Oh Scooter what you been doing? Boy what you think you been doing? Now you going somewhere talking about you been doing that with a big girl now ain't you? Now tell the truth. Because that's all right with me. Because you better not tell nobody who it was just like you wouldn't tell me on little old skinny butt Charlene Wingate.

Boy Scooter, she said not only pointing but aiming her finger at me with one eye closed, Boy if you tell somebody on me boy you sure going to wish you hadn't when I get through with you. Boy you go somewhere and tell somebody something like this on me and I will natural born fix you sonny boy and I mean it Scooter and if you don't believe it just go on somewhere and say something and see. Because you know what I'm going to do I'm going to say you didn't do nothing but come up there acting just like some little old daddy fyce puppy dog and all I did was start to laughing and laughed you right on out of here. I declare I will. I declare before God I will Scooter.

But then she was also grinning as if for both of us again, and she pushed me and said: I just said that. You know I just said that don't you Scooter? You know I just said that just to see because you already know you all right with me don't you Scooter?

The next time was that day coming through Skin Game Jungle on the way back from taking the twelve o'clock basket to Mr. Paul Miles at Blue Rock mill when she said Hey wait a minute Scooter because I got to squat. Hey ain't you got to do something too? Hey I bet you something. Hey you know what I bet you? I bet you you still ain't got nothing down there but your thing. I bet you you ain't even starting in to sprout your first fuzz yet. Now tell the truth now Scooter. That's how come you shamed to pee now ain't it?

She said That's all right about your thing. Ain't nobody talking about that. I'm talking about some hairs. I'm talking about what I'm doing doing something like that with some little old boy ain't even old enough to do nothing but some dog water. Because when you first start to have to shave with a sure enough razor and lather that's how you know when a boy already getting to be a man enough to make a baby. That's what I'm talking about. I'm talking about some sure enough doing it like some sure enough grown folks with your hair mingling together and all that and then the man shoot off. That's what I'm talking about.

But that was also the time when she said: What you standing there holding yourself looking at me like that for. Come on boy because that's all right about that just this one more time.

The time after that, which was that day while Mama and Miss Tee were up in Chickasaw with Miss Liza Jefferson, was my first time in a real bed with no clothes on, and she said I'm going to show you something this time, and she did. She said I bet you you don't even know what that is. That's just the old Georgia grind, and this the gritty grind. I bet you you ain't never done the sporty grind before. She said This the bobo and this the sporty bobo and this the whip and this the bullwhip and this the snatch. She said When the man put his legs like that with his arms like that he straddling the mountain and the woman can do the greasy pole and when the woman put up her self like this that mean the man can come to the buck and when me and you go like this that's what you call bumping the stump.

She said When you see me doing this that's when I'm doing my belly roll to sell my jelly roll. Like Miss Sweetmeat

Thompson. Like Miss Big Money Watkins. Then she said What you going do when I sic my puppies on you like Miss Slick McGinnis all the way out in San Fransisco? and I said Sic them back that's all right who like. Because I couldn't make up my mind whether I wanted to be like Stagolee or Luzana Cholly or Elmore Sanders. And that's when she said Well let me see you sic them then and started snapping her fingers and sucking her breath through her teeth.

I don't remember when I uncrossed my fingers that time. All I have ever been able to recollect about what happened next is hearing her whisper Oh shit oh hell oh goddamn and then saying Oh shit now oh hell now oh goddamn now Scooter. And suddenly I was not sure that I was not about to begin to spurt blood from somewhere in the very center of my being and I didn't even care. Because in that same instant it was as if you were coming through the soft stream-warm velvet gates to the most secret place in the world, and I had to keep on doing what I was doing no matter what happened.

And I did. By reaching and by holding and by floating and by pushing and by slipping and sliding and slittering and by hithering and by thithering through cinnamon scented sardine oil and dog fennel thickets and dog fennel meadows.

Then afterwards she said What did I tell you? Didn't I tell you? Oh Scooter see there? Oh Scooter you little rascal you just now losing your cherry. Scooter boy you done lost your cherry just like I told you. What did I tell you? I told you about messing around with big girls now didn't I? Oh Scooter you done lost your cherry and I bet you I know who the one took it.

The one who wrote: *Dear SP guess who (smile) you are my SP because you so cute and also sweet from X guess who (smile) XXX is for hug and kisses for smiles (smile)*, was Elva Lois Showers, who was also the one who started saying Please don't now stop that now as soon as I touched her arm. Please don't please don't. Not now Scooter. Now boy you better stop. You better stop that now Scooter.

Please don't what, I said.

You know what, she said You know good and well what. Just behave yourself. Just don't be doing nothing trying to do that. How come you cain't just be nice, Scooter?

That was when we were in the eighth grade and her seat was three rows over and she answered the roll call after *Ross, J. T.* and before *Singleton, Fred Douglass.* So I knew whose handwriting it was as soon as I unfolded the note, because that was also when everybody used to have to go to the blackboard to write sentences almost as often as you used to have to go work problems in arithmetic. I didn't look over that way for the rest of that afternoon, and I could hardly wait for the last bell so I could be all to myself and read it again.

I felt good thinking and whistling about it all the way home, and I went to sleep thinking about it and I woke thinking and whistling about it. But all I did when I got back to school was act as if nothing had happened. So I worried all the way home that next day and spent that night wondering what you were supposed to do, but then the day after that every time I had to stand up to recite I felt that good, warm, feathery-light way you feel when you realize (without having to look) that somebody is looking at you because she has been thinking about you.

Which is why on the way out for twelve o'clock recess I got to the door at the same time as she did and said what I said. I said Hello. (Not only like a big boy but also like a big schoolboy. All I had ever said to her or to any other girl before was Hey. Hey Elva Lois what you know. Hey Elva Lois what you doing. Hey Elva Lois girl where you been. Where you going.) I said Hello and she turned up her nose and ran on out to the girls' play area behind Willie Mae Crawford before I could even say Elva Lois. But that next morning there was another note: S is for secret and P is for passion (smile) F is for how come you try to be so fresh (smile).

So that was the day I carried her books as far as the Hill-side Store for the first time, and all I did was say Bye and came back whistling and the next day there was the next note: *Thinking of somebody very very sweet guess who (smile) XXX kisses (smile)*. But as soon as I did what I did that next time she said what she said and pulled away and ran half way down Martin's Lane before she turned and blew lilac time kisses at me from both hands before going through the gate.

The next time and the time after that and the time after that and so forth she also said and said and said: How come you always got to come getting so fresh with somebody, Scooter? Boy, I'm telling you. That's all you think about. How come you can't just be my SP and be nice? How come every time we get somewhere like this you always got to start acting like that? I'm talking about every time, Scooter. I'm talking about every time. Everytime we somewhere out of sight. Everytime we happen to come by some old empty house or something. Everytime we somewhere and it start to get dark. And don't let it start to raining.

There was also the time when she said: How come you can't just be nice like in class? That's when you so smart and neat and everybody always talking about you so cute, and come to find you just as big a devil as you can be, Scooter. Boy, I'm telling you; you sure got Miss Lexine Metcalf fooled. You and David Lovett. That's all he think about too. Just like you. That's what Clarice say and I sure can believe it now. Scooter y'all think y'all something just because Miss Lexine Metcalf think y'all so smart, don't you? Y'all think somebody supposed to let you do that just because she always talking about you and him the two main boys know your homework so good all the time. Well let me tell you something. Don't nobody care nothing about what no Miss Lexine Metcalf say, Scooter.

Because she just makes me so sick carrying on like that about some little old fresh boys like you and little old David Lovett anyhow. Because she ain't doing nothing but giving y'all the big head nohow. Because that's exactly how come y'all think y'all so cute somebody supposed let y'all do something like that any time you want to. Especially you, Scooter. Just because some old Miss Lexine Metcalf talking about you going to amount to something so important some of these days.

If that's the way you feel, I said. If that's how you want to be, Elva Lois.

Now that ain't what I said, Scooter, she said. Ain't nobody said nothing about that. You don't even know what I'm talking about. You might know how to get your lesson but that don't mean you know something about what girls talking about. You don't know nothing about no girls, boy.

Then she promised. And I almost believed her. Because that was when she said: Sure enough now Scooter. But not right now Scooter. Not this time Scooter. I got to go now Scooter. I got to be back home now. Didn't I say I would? I already told you, Scooter. This not fair for you to come trying to do that when I already told you. See that's what I'm talking about. And I already said I would.

But she never did. Because what she said that next time was I promised you and now you supposed to promise me something too. And when I said That's not what you said, she said I don't care what I said that's what I meant, because that's what I always meant. When the girl say yes, you supposed to do what she say first, Scooter.

So that was all that ever became of me and Elva Lois Showers that spring which I also remember because the song that was featured during the baseball games was "Precious Little Thing Called Love." Because I was not about to cut my finger and swear by my blood. Not me. I said I don't care Elva Lois. I said That's all right with me because I don't care.

Shoot goddamn right, Little Buddy said when I told him about it that same night. Shoot man what she think this is. Shoot Elva Lois Showers. Shooot she all right but she ain't all that pretty. Shooot tell her she crazy, man. Shoot tell her that's what the goddamn hell SP suppose to mean, some you know what. Secret just meant on the QT. Shoot tell her if she won't, somegoddamnbody else sure will. Elva Lois Showers. Shoot. Man I just can't get over that heifer. Elva Lois Showers. Goddamn. Shoot.

One somebody else who always would on the QT was Beulah Chaney (who should have been at least two grades ahead of me at that time but whose seat was by the window in the first row behind Walter Lee Cauldwell). She was the one who said I got something for you, Scooter, that day at the blackboard while everybody else was outside for Maypole practice.

I ain't going tell you what because if you don't already

know that's just too bad. If somebody got to tell you that, all I can say you not old enough yet. So if you want me to give it to you you got to come where I say when I say.

She lived at the edge of Chickasabogue Bottom. To get there you had to go along the AT & N toward Chickasaw until you came to Blue Poplar Crossing. Then you cut through that part of Parker's Mill Quarters to the elderberry corner and came all the way down the three-quarter mile winding slope, and you could see the barn and the wood-shed under the moss draped trees beyond the open wagon gate.

Well I declare Scooter, she said that first time, Here you all the way over here sure enough. Boy what if I just said that just to see? What if I just said that just to see if I could fool you to come way over here?

But she had not. She was surprised but anybody could see how pleased she also was, and before I could stop grinning long enough to put on my frown and say Oh Beulah Chaney, she said Come on Scooter. I'm just teasing. You know I'm just teasing you, don't you Scooter? That mean I must like you Scooter. Because when you like somebody, look like you just have to be teasing them and all of that just because you might be kinda glad to see them or something.

But later on in the plum thickets beyond the collard patch (with everybody away because it was Saturday afternoon) she was only half teasing: Oh Scooter I'm surprised at you. I'm talking about you just as sneaky as you can be. How you know this what I was talking about? I coulda been talking about a lost ball I found or something like a mitt or something like that. I coulda been talking about some books and things I found in the bottom of the trunk or something and here you come with this the first thing on your mind just like everybody else just because I said that. You ought to be shamed of yourself Scooter. Now tell the truth ain't you shamed of yourself all the way over here doing something like this?

As if you didn't already know what would start if anybody even so much as suspected that you had ever been there: Hey Scooter where Beulah Chaney? Hey Scooter Beulah Chaney looking for you, man. Hey Scooter Beulah Chaney say come there, man. Hey Scooter Beulah Chaney say she sure do miss you since that last time you come down in the bottom. She say hurry up back. Hey Scooter guess who they say your girl now? Old Beulah Chaney. Hey Scooter here come your new girl. Old big bottom beulah chaney old pillow busom beulah chaney loping like a milk cow. Hey Scooter you know what she say? She say she got something for you. She say she got some more for you man.

Not that you didn't know there was another side to it all. Because even as they said what they had said to try to scandalize me in front of everybody in the schoolyard during ten o'clock recess that time you could tell that something else was bothering them. And sooner or later somebody was going to bring it up in one way or another (especially somebody two or three grades ahead of you): Hey what some little old scooter butt booty butt squirt like you doing hanging around some old big ass tough ass heifer like Beulah Chaney for? Boy you know what they tell me? They say you over there trying to mind that old funky pussy. They say you ain't nothing but some little old granny-dodging cock knocker, Scooter. So whyn't you just look out the goddamn way, junior? Look out the way and let somebody over in there know how to handle that stuff. Hey you want somebody to show you how to handle some big old heifer like that? Well don't be looking at me because somebody might find out.

Me myself I don't care, she said. Because you think I don't know what they always trying to say about somebody? You think I don't know they always behind somebody's back trying to make some kind of old fun of somebody and calling somebody all them old names. You think don't nobody know what they doing every time they come running up in my face saying something just to see what I'm going say so they can go back somewhere and laugh some more? They think somebody so dumb. They the one dumb.

You the one got everybody fooled. You the one always going around like you so nice you don't never think about nothing like this because you ain't never got no time for nothing but studying something in some of them old books for Miss

Lexine Metcalf and here you over here just as soon as I told you something like that.

Calling somebody riney, she said another time, I ain't no riney and they know it. I might be this color, but that don't make nobody no riney. Because look at my hair and look at somebody like old nappy headed Jessie Mae Blount. Ain't nothing on me that red and nappy, and she even got all them freckles and splotches, and ain't nobody never been going around calling her nothing like that. So that's all right with me if they got to say something. Because I don't care. But anytime they come trying to make out like they cain't stand to be getting next to me without turning up their nose and that kind of stuff, that ain't fair. Because some of them might got a few pretty clothes but that don't mean cain't nobody else be just as neat and clean.

She was more yaller than riney and her hair was more of a curly brown than a kinky red and her eyes were blue-green. So what with her living that close to Chickasabogue Swamp and what with her gray-eyed father being a raft man and a boom man who also had a whiskey still somewhere up in Hog Bayou and what with her tallow faced mother (on those rare times you glimpsed her) almost always wearing a bonnet and an apron like somebody from Citronelle or Chastang, Little Buddy and I always took it for granted that she was probably more Cajun than anything else.

What she mostly smelled like was green moss. But that

first time it was willow branches then fig branches then plum leaves. Sometimes it was sweetgum leaves plus sweetgum sap. And sometimes it was green pine needles plus pine trunk bark plus turpentine-box rosin. But mainly it was live oak twigs which she chewed plus Spanish moss which she used to make a ground pallet.

She said: Anybody say I ain't just as clean as the next one just plain telling a big old something-ain't-so. Anybody come talking like I might got something somebody subject to be catching from me they just trying to start something about somebody. Like cain't nobody get them back if I want to. You just let them keep on and see. Somebody always trying to think they so much better than somebody. They ain't no better than nobody else. If they think somebody think they better than somebody they must be crazy. Because don't think don't nobody know nothing on every last one of them.

On the other hand there was also Johnnie Mae Lewis with her johnnie mae lewis long legs and her johnnie mae neat waist and her johnnie mae knee stockings and her johnnie mae prompt princess tapered A-plus recitation fingers and her johnnie mae perfect penmanship who not only said Not me not you Scooter in front of everybody standing by the punch bowl table that afterschool partytime and not only refused my hand before I could get it up but then danced off with Sonny Kemble of all the knuckleheads that I had always thought she wouldn't even speak to and to "Little White Lies" of all the rain sad honeysuckle melodies that I was forever whistling when I was alone with my boy-blue expectations and my steel-blue determination that spring the year before Beulah Chaney.

Nor have I forgotten Maecile Cheatham and her chocolate brown dimples and her glossy creek indian black pocahontas braids, who tricked me into saying what I said so she could go back and tell Claribel Owens who said You think you so slick don't you Scooter you go to be so smart and don't even know better than to try to do something like that with somebody's best friend and I'm talking about the very one that already said that's all you trying to see if you can do. I'm talking about the very one already told me about you and Ardelle Foster and you and Julia Glover and you and Evelyn Childs too Mister think you so much and ain't shit Scooter so good bye.

Then that time which is also the baseball spring and summer I remember whenever no matter wherever I hear downhome trombones tailgating "At Sundown" there was also Olivet Dixon with her big bold olivet dixon eyes and her big bold olivet dixon legs and hips and her underslung olivet rubber doll dixon walk that made her seem two or even three years older than I was instead of one year younger. She was the one who said: The one I like is Melvin Porter because he don't have to always be trying to be some little teacher's pet.

Melvin Porter is a real sport. Melvin Porter dress like a real sheik. Melvin Porter is the one all the girls like because he got experience.

melvin porter

melvin porter

melvin porter

melvin porter

He got it and gone all over you any day Scooter. He got experience over you Scooter.

So I said Well good for melvin porter okay for melvin porter hooray for melvin porter melvin porter melvin porter who was the mean sixteen I was still that far away from. Who got her in the family way and hopped a sundown freight train for Los Angeles, California and left her to John Wesley Griffin who was seventeen and who quit school and married her and went to work at Shypes Planer Mill and then lost her to Wendell Robinson who was twenty and was a bellboy downtown at the Battle House and took her to dances on Davis Avenue and got her that way again and went to Chicago and did not send back for her.

The one I remember when I remember crape myrtle yard blossoms is Charlene Wingate, to whom I said what I said when she said You suppose to say roses red and violets blue and you suppose to tell me Charlene I love you and you suppose to ask me Charlene be my valentine and you suppose to call me baby and you suppose to say I'm your sugar and when you say you my sweet one and only you suppose to cross your heart Scooter because when you tell somebody something like that that's when you suppose to promise.

I do Charlene, I said.

And she said I'm talking about sure enough now Scooter because I'm talking about when somebody want somebody to be sweethearts.

And I said Me too Charlene.

And she said Well then.

And I looked at her and her Creole frizzy hair and her honey brown face and her crape myrtle blossom smile and waited.

And she said All you said was you do Scooter do what Scooter you suppose to say it Scooter that's the way you suppose to do.

And that was the very first time I ever said that in my life and that was when she said Well you know what the boy suppose to do when the girl say here I stand on two little chips. And I said Come and kiss your two sweet lips. And that is what I did without even thinking about it. And that was when she said You suppose to whisper darling and you suppose to whisper honey because now we suppose to be sweethearts Scooter.

Which was also when she said When you sweethearts that's when you have sweet heartaches every time you just think about somebody and every time you just hear somebody say that name you have to hold yourself to keep somebody from seeing you looking and when you know you going to be somewhere at the same time you cain't hardly wait and when you see somebody coming and it look like the one you want it to be you have to catch your breath because that's your weakness.

Then when she said How you miss me Scooter how much you think about me, I said A whole lot Charlene. But I never did what Little Buddy Marshall used to do when he was thinking about Estelle Saunders. Because not only did he used to say Yes sir that's my baby you know don't mean maybe, but sometimes he also used to limp-walk straddling his right hand while swinging his left arm scat singing Has she got da, de da yes she has got dadeda that certain that certain body do she like do de do yes she like my dodedo that certain body of mine.

What I said that first time in the crape myrtle playhouse was If we suppose to be playing house we suppose to you know Charlene, and she said First you suppose to go to work Scooter and then I'm suppose to bring you your dinner basket and then you suppose to come home and eat supper and then we suppose to sit in the parlor and then you suppose to stand up and stretch because you ready to go to bed. And then Scooter. That's when Scooter.

• • •

The Gins Alley victrola music I remember when I remember Deljean McCray all dressed up and on her way somewhere walking like Creola Calloway and like Miss Slick McGinnis as Little Buddy Marshall and I myself used to walk like Luzana Cholly and also like Stagolee Dupas is Jelly Roll Morton and the Red Hot Peppers playing "Kansas City Stomp" as if in the pre-game grandstand with the pre-game pennants flying and the vendors hawking pre-game peanuts, popcorn, ice cream, candy, hot dogs and barbecue sandwiches, and the circus elephant tuba carrying all the way out to the dog fennels beyond the outfield.

But the song I remember when I remember her snapping her fingers and rolling her stomach and snatching her hips and pouting her lips and winking and rolling her eyes at the same time is "How Come You Do Me Like You Do." And she also used to like to sing "Ja-Da" and You got to hmmm sweet mama or you won't see mama at all. As if she never even heard of the Deljean McCray who was as concerned as it turned out she always was about Miss Tee. About whom she was also the one who said Boy Scooter if she ever find out about me being the one been doing something like this with you every time her back turn boy I just know she subject to just about kill me Scooter. Boy I rather for Miss Melba to be the one any day. And I'm talking about Miss Tee so nice I don't believe she even want to kill a flea. But boy Scooter I just know that woman subject to beat my ass till my nose bleed if she ever find out about me spoiling you like this. Because everybody know how much she like children especially little old frisky tail boys think they so smart. Because you know what folks say? They say she had her heart set on being a schoolteacher like Miss Lexine Metcalf and Miss Kell and Miss Norris and them. That's how come she got all them books and pretty things and all them flowers and keep her house painted and her fence whitewashed like that. Because all that come from way back when she used to be off in training before she come down here on a visit and ended up getting married to my uncle Paul Boykin. So that's how that happened. Because Uncle Paul said that was that about all of that. So that's when she had to give up on it. And then come to find out they don't look like they going to even get no children of her own for her to bring up with all the schooling she still got.

That's how come she so crazy about children, she also said. And that's how come children so crazy about her. Because she just like a good teacher because that's the way she talk and she can tell you all about different things and show them all them different games and you don't have to be sitting up in no classroom scared somebody just up there waiting for you to make a mistake or something. Like that Miss booty butt Kell with her booty butt self.

But boy Scooter you the favorite one she like over all of us around here and I'm suppose to be in the family. And I bet

you I know how come. You know how come? You want me to
tell you how come you the one her natural born pet and don't
care who knows it. Them books. Because you the one take to
them books like that's your birthmark or something Scooter.
And that's what she like better than anything in this world and
here you come just as smart as you devilish. And you know it
too son. And don't tell me you don't know you her heart. Ain't
nothing she got too good for you and you know it. And you
know something else I bet you if Miss Melba and Unka Whit
let her she would flat out adopt you boy. Everybody know
that. Boy Scooter she give anything to get her hands on you
for her own. That's how come I just know she'll cold kill me
if she ever was to find out about something like this. Because
you know she bound to put it all on me just like you didn't
have nothing in the world to do with it.

When I came back for Christmas that time and saw her
working behind the counter when I went into Smallwoods
Cleaning and Pressing Club she said Mister College Boy. Well
all right Mister College Boy. Well go on Mister College Boy.
Well excuse me Mister College Boy and I said Come on Deljean. I said How you been Deljean. I said I been thinking
about you Deljean. I been wondering what you doing. And
she said You the one Scooter. She said You the one better go
on out of here. Boy you know good and well you not up there
with all them high class college girls thinking about somebody

like me. Boy, Scooter, used to be little old Scooter, tell the truth now, you forgot all about me up there now didn't you? Boy you ain't thought about me until just you walked in here and seen me just now. And I said That's what you say Deljean. That's what you say.

I said How could somebody ever forget you Deljean. I said you know something? I don't even have to think about you Deljean to remember you. Just like I don't have to think of Little Buddy and Luzana Cholly and Stagolee and Gator Gus and all that. Because that's the way you really remember somebody. I said You the one got my cherry Deljean. I said You remember that time. I said You the one taught me what it's made for Deljean. I said You the one used to keep me out of a whole lot of trouble Deljean.

I said Ain't no telling what kind of mess I mighta got all tangled up in if it hadn't been for you Deljean. And she said Boy Scooter boy you a lying dog. That ain't the way I heard it. Boy who you think you coming in here trying to fool. Because I know exactly who that was from the tenth grade on. You think don't nobody know about you and her. And right under Miss Tee's nose and she so glad you making all them good marks and winning all them scholarship prizes and stuff up there in high school she ain't even suspected it to this day. But see me myself I know you Scooter. I mighta been married and having that baby for that old no good nigger but I bet you I can tell you just about everything you call yourself doing in them days. I bet you. I even know about you and old big butt Beulah Chaney, Scooter, and I know you didn't know nobody know about that. Because you know what? As soon as I seen you coming out from down over in there one time and I said to myself old Scooter think he so slick but he cain't fool me. Because I know you Scooter, at least I used to know you. Because I don't know nothing about no college boys.

But she also said: Boy Scooter if you ain't still a mess. Here we doing this again. And she said Boy I'm surprised at you Scooter. You suppose to be a college boy. I thought college boys suppose to be so proper. I thought college boys suppose to be so dictified. I thought college boys suppose to be such a gentleman all the time.

That was that next evening. And she also said Well all right Mister College Boy. Well go on then. I see you. You think you something don't you. I didn't teach you that. Did she teach you that. You know who I'm talking about. Didn't no high class college girls teach you that. And that was when she said Boy Scooter Miss Tee sure subject to come over here and kill me if she find out her precious Mister College Boy over here putting in time with this old used to be married woman that didn't go no further than the ninth grade. Specially after all she done for me.

She said: Boy Scooter Miss Tee so proud you up there getting all that good education she don't know what to do.

That's all she talk about every chance she get. She still just as nice to me as she can be just like she always was. Just like ain't nothing happened. Except keeping Twenty for me so I can work since I made that old no good nigger get his old lazy ass out of here and he finally went on up north somewhere. But you still the one her heart Scooter. And that's the way she want Twenty to be too. Just like you. You seen Twenty over there. That's what they call him. For Quinty. Because his name Quinten Roosevelt. Quinten Roosevelt Hopson. He five and Boy if he turn out to like his books he got him a home with Miss Tee don't care what happen to me. Boy she cain't hardly wait to send him to school so he can get on up there and come by Miss Metcalf like you. With your used to be little old go-to-be-so-slick self. But you was born marked for it Scooter.

The last time with Deljean McCray was that night after the Mardi Gras parade when I came back during that war for that special occasion. It was that many years after college then, and she said Look at me with these three children now and getting almost big as a house. And look at you Scooter used to be that little old think-you-so-smart-and-cute schoolboy I used to could make him blush anytime I want to. And I said You still can Deljean. I said What you think I'm doing right now. And she said You something else Scooter. She said You always been something else Scooter and that's how come you always been all right with me almost as bad as Miss Tee. And that was when she said That's the only part that make me feel sorry about all this happening today. Because she not here to see you come back this time. Because I can just see her looking at her mister so proud she can hardly stand it. But that's how come you still all right with me too Scooter. Because that's something everybody got to give you your credit for. Because the one thing she didn't never have to worry about right on up to her dying day was you trying your best to make somebody out of yourself.

Which is also when she also said: You know something Scooter. Boy you never could fool me. I'm the one fooled you Scooter. You remember that time when I was the one that got your cherry. Well you suppose to be the one so smart and I bet you a fat man you didn't know that's when you got mine too until I just now told you.

from

WINESBURG, OHIO

SHERWOOD ANDERSON

These famous closing chapters from Sherwood
Anderson's masterpiece put words to the silent and
breathtaking dance that can happen when a boy
and girl help each other into their futures.

SOPHISTICATION

It was early evening of a day in the late fall and the Winesburg County Fair had brought crowds of country people into town. The day had been clear and the night came on warm and pleasant. On the Trunion Pike, where the road after it left town stretched away between berry fields now covered with dry brown leaves, the dust from passing wagons arose in clouds. Children, curled into little balls, slept on the straw scattered on wagon beds. Their hair was full of dust and their fingers black and sticky. The dust rolled away over the fields and the departing sun set it ablaze with colors.

In the main street of Winesburg crowds filled the stores and the sidewalks. Night came on, horses whinnied, the clerks in the stores ran madly about, children became lost and cried lustily, an American town worked terribly at the task of amusing itself.

Pushing his way through the crowds in Main Street, young George Willard concealed himself in the stairway leading to Doctor Reefy's office and looked at the people. With feverish eyes he watched the faces drifting past under the store lights. Thoughts kept coming into his head and he did not want to think. He stamped impatiently on the wooden steps and looked sharply about. "Well, is she going to stay with him all day? Have I done all this waiting for nothing?" he muttered.

George Willard, the Ohio village boy, was fast growing into manhood and new thoughts had been coming into his mind. All that day, amid the jam of people at the Fair, he had gone about feeling lonely. He was about to leave Winesburg to go away to some city where he hoped to get work on a city newspaper and he felt grown up. The mood that had taken possession of him was a thing known to men and unknown to boys. He felt old and a little tired. Memories awoke in him. To his mind his new sense of maturity set him apart, made of him a half-tragic figure. He wanted someone to understand the feeling that had taken possession of him after his mother's death.

There is a time in the life of every boy when he for the first time takes the backward view of life. Perhaps that is the moment when he crosses the line into manhood. The boy is walking through the street of his town. He is thinking of the future and of the figure he will cut in the world. Ambitions and regrets awake within him. Suddenly something happens; he stops under a tree and waits as for a voice calling his name. Ghosts of old things creep into his consciousness; the voices outside of himself whisper a message concerning the limitations of life. From being quite sure of himself and his future he becomes not at all sure. If he be an imaginative boy a door is torn open and for the first time he looks out upon the world, seeing, as though they marched in procession before him, the countless figures of men who before his time have come out of nothingness into the world, lived their lives and again disappeared into nothingness. The sadness of sophistication has come to the boy. With a little gasp he sees himself as merely a leaf blown by the wind through the streets of his village. He knows that in spite of all the stout talk of his fellows he must live and die in uncertainty, a thing blown by the winds, a thing destined like corn to wilt in the sun. He shivers and looks eagerly about. The eighteen years he has lived seem but a moment, a breathing space in the long march of humanity. Already he hears death calling. With all his heart he wants to come close to some other human, touch someone with his hands, be touched by the hand of another. If he prefers that the other be a woman, that is because he believes that a woman will be gentle, that she will understand. He wants, most of all, understanding.

When the moment of sophistication came to George Willard his mind turned to Helen White, the Winesburg banker's daughter. Always he had been conscious of the girl growing into womanhood as he grew into manhood. Once on a summer night when he was eighteen, he had walked with her on a country road and in her presence had given way to an impulse to boast, to make himself appear big and significant in her eyes. Now he wanted to see her for another purpose. He wanted to tell her of the new impulses that had come to him. He had tried to make her think of him as a man when he knew nothing of manhood and now he wanted to be with her and to try to make her feel the change he believed had taken place in his nature.

As for Helen White, she also had come to a period of change. What George felt, she in her young woman's way felt also. She was no longer a girl and hungered to reach into the grace and beauty of womanhood. She had come home from Cleveland, where she was attending college, to spend a day at the Fair. She also had begun to have memories. During the day she sat in the grand-stand with a young man, one of the instructors from the college, who was a guest of her mother's. The young man was of a pedantic turn of mind and she felt at once he would not do for her purpose. At the Fair she was glad to be seen in his company as he was well dressed and a stranger. She knew that the fact of his presence would create an impression. During the day she was happy, but when night came on she began to grow restless. She wanted to drive the instructor away, to get out of his presence. While they sat together in the grand-stand and while the eyes of former schoolmates were upon them, she paid so much attention to her escort that he grew interested. "A scholar needs money. I should marry a woman with money," he mused.

Helen White was thinking of George Willard even as he wandered gloomily through the crowds thinking of her. She remembered the summer evening when they had walked together and wanted to walk with him again. She thought that the months she had spent in the city, the going to theaters and the seeing of great crowds wandering in lighted thoroughfares, had changed her profoundly. She wanted him to feel and be conscious of the change in her nature.

The summer evening together that had left its mark on the memory of both the young man and woman had, when looked at quite sensibly, been rather stupidly spent. They had walked out of town along a country road. Then they had stopped by a fence near a field of young corn and George had taken off his coat and let it hang on his arm. "Well, I've stayed here in Winesburg—yes—I've not yet gone away but I'm growing up," he had said. "I've been reading books and I've been thinking. I'm going to try to amount to something in life.

"Well," he explained, "that isn't the point. Perhaps I'd better quit talking."

The confused boy put his hand on the girl's arm. His voice trembled. The two started to walk back along the road toward town. In his desperation George boasted, "I'm going to be a big man, the biggest that ever lived here in Winesburg," he declared. "I want you to do something, I don't know what. Perhaps it is none of my business. I want you to try to be different from other women. You see the point. It's none of my business I tell you. I want you to be a beautiful woman. You see what I want."

The boy's voice failed and in silence the two came back into town and went along the street to Helen White's house. At the gate he tried to say something impressive. Speeches he had thought out came into his head, but they seemed utterly pointless. "I thought—I used to think—I had it in my mind you would marry Seth Richmond. Now I know you won't," was all he could find to say as she went through the gate and toward the door of her house.

On the warm fall evening as he stood in the stairway and looked at the crowd drifting through Main Street, George thought of the talk beside the field of young corn and was ashamed of the figure he had made of himself. In the street the people surged up and down like cattle confined in a pen. Buggies and wagons almost filled the narrow thoroughfare. A band played and small boys raced along the sidewalk, diving between the legs of men. Young men with shining red faces walked awkwardly about with girls on their arms. In a room above one of the stores, where a dance was to be held, the fiddlers tuned their instruments. The broken sounds floated down through an open window and out across the murmur of voices and the loud blare of the horns of the band. The medley of sounds got on young Willard's nerves. Everywhere, on all sides, the sense of crowding, moving life closed in about him. He wanted to run away by himself and think. "If she wants to stay with that fellow she may. Why should I care? What difference does it make to me?" he growled and went along Main Street and through Hern's Grocery into a side street.

George felt so utterly lonely and dejected that he wanted to weep but pride made him walk rapidly along, swinging his arms. He came to Wesley Moyer's livery barn and stopped in the shadows to listen to a group of men who talked of a race Wesley's stallion, Tony Tip, had won at the Fair during the afternoon. A crowd had gathered in front of the barn and before the crowd walked Wesley, prancing up and down and boasting. He held a whip in his hand and kept tapping the ground. Little puffs of dust arose in the lamplight. "Hell, quit your talking," Wesley exclaimed. "I wasn't afraid, I knew I had 'em beat all the time. I wasn't afraid."

Ordinarily George Willard would have been intensely interested in the boasting of Moyer, the horseman. Now it made him angry. He turned and hurried away along the street. "Old windbag," he sputtered. "Why does he want to be bragging? Why don't he shut up?"

George went into a vacant lot and, as he hurried along, fell over a pile of rubbish. A nail protruding from an empty barrel tore his trousers. He sat down on the ground and swore. With a pin he mended the torn place and then arose and went on. "I'll go to Helen White's house, that's what I'll do. I'll walk right in. I'll say that I want to see her. I'll walk right in and sit down, that's what I'll do," he declared, climbing over a fence and beginning to run.

• • •

On the veranda of Banker White's house Helen was restless and distraught. The instructor sat between the mother and daughter. His talk wearied the girl. Although he had also been raised in an Ohio town, the instructor began to put on the airs of the city. He wanted to appear cosmopolitan. "I like the chance you have given me to study the background out of which most of our girls come," he declared. "It was good of you, Mrs. White, to have me down for the day." He turned to Helen and laughed. "Your life is still bound up with the life of this town?" he asked. "There are people here in whom you are interested?" To the girl his voice sounded pompous and heavy.

Helen arose and went into the house. At the door leading to a garden at the back she stopped and stood listening. Her mother began to talk. "There is no one here fit to associate with a girl of Helen's breeding," she said.

Helen ran down a flight of stairs at the back of the house and into the garden. In the darkness she stopped and stood trembling. It seemed to her that the world was full of meaningless people saying words. Afire with eagerness she ran through a garden gate and, turning a corner by the banker's barn, went into a little side street. "George! Where are you, George?" she cried, filled with nervous excitement. She stopped running, and leaned against a tree to laugh hysterically. Along the dark little street came George Willard, still saying words. "I'm going to walk right into her house. I'll go right in and sit down," he declared as he came up to her. He stopped and stared stupidly. "Come on," he said and took hold of her hand. With hanging heads they walked away along the street under the trees. Dry leaves rustled under foot. Now that he had found her George wondered what he had better do and say.

At the upper end of the Fair Ground, in Winesburg, there is a half decayed old grand-stand. It has never been painted and the boards are all warped out of shape. The Fair Ground stands on top of a low hill rising out of the valley of Wine Creek and from the grand-stand one can see at night, over a cornfield, the lights of the town reflected against the sky.

George and Helen climbed the hill to the Fair Ground, coming by the path past Waterworks Pond. The feeling of loneliness and isolation that had come to the young man in the crowded streets of his town was both broken and intensified by the presence of Helen. What he felt was reflected in her.

In youth there are always two forces fighting in people. The warm unthinking little animal struggles against the thing that reflects and remembers, and the older, the more sophisticated thing had possession of George Willard. Sensing his mood, Helen walked beside him filled with respect. When they got to the grand-stand they climbed up under the roof and sat down on one of the long bench-like seats.

There is something memorable in the experience to be had by going into a fair ground that stands at the edge of a Middle Western town on a night after the annual fair has been held. The sensation is one never to be forgotten. On all sides are ghosts, not of the dead, but of living people. Here, during the day just passed, have come the people pouring in from the town and the country around. Farmers with their wives and children and all the people from the hundreds of little frame houses have gathered within these board walls. Young girls have laughed and men with beards have talked of the affairs of their lives. The place has been filled to overflowing with life. It has itched and squirmed with life and now it is night and the life has all gone away. The silence is almost terrifying. One conceals oneself standing silently beside the trunk of a tree and what there is of a reflective tendency in his nature is intensified. One shudders at the thought of the meaninglessness of life while at the same instant, and if the people of the town are his people, one loves life so intensely that tears come into the eyes.

In the darkness under the roof of the grand-stand, George Willard sat beside Helen White and felt very keenly his own insignificance in the scheme of existence. Now that he had come out of town where the presence of the people stirring about, busy with a multitude of affairs, had been so irritating, the irritation was all gone. The presence of Helen renewed and refreshed him. It was as though her woman's hand was assisting him to make some minute readjustment of the machinery of his life. He began to think of the people in the town where he had always lived with something like reverence. He had reverence for Helen. He wanted to love and to be loved by her, but he did not want at the moment to be confused by her womanhood. In the darkness he took hold of her hand and when she crept close put a hand on her shoulder. A wind began to blow and he shivered. With all his strength he tried to hold and to understand the mood that had come upon him. In that high place in the darkness the two oddly sensitive human atoms held each other tightly and waited. In the mind of each was the same thought. "I have come to this lonely place and here is this other," was the substance of the thing felt.

In Winesburg the crowded day had run itself out into the long night of the late fall. Farm horses jogged away along lonely country roads pulling their portion of weary people. Clerks began to bring samples of goods in off the sidewalks and lock the doors of stores. In the Opera House a crowd had gathered to see a show and further down Main Street the fiddlers, their instruments tuned, sweated and worked to keep the feet of youth flying over a dance floor.

In the darkness in the grand-stand Helen White and George Willard remained silent. Now and then the spell that held them was broken and they turned and tried in the dim light to see into each other's eyes. They kissed but that impulse did not last. At the upper end of the Fair Ground a half dozen men worked over horses that had raced during the afternoon. The men had built a fire and were heating kettles of water. Only their legs could be seen as they passed back and forth in the light. When the wind blew the little flames of the fire danced crazily about.

George and Helen arose and walked away into the darkness. They went along a path past a field of corn that had not yet been cut. The wind whispered among the dry corn blades. For a moment during the walk back into town the spell that held them was broken. When they had come to the crest of Waterworks Hill they stopped by a tree and George again put his hands on the girl's shoulders. She embraced him eagerly and then again they drew quickly back from that impulse. They stopped kissing and stood a little apart. Mutual respect grew big in them. They were both embarrassed and to relieve their embarrassment dropped into the animalism of youth. They laughed and began to pull and haul at each other. In some way chastened and purified by the mood they had been in, they became, not man and woman, not boy and girl, but excited little animals.

It was so they went down the hill. In the darkness they played like two splendid young things in a young world. Once, running swiftly forward, Helen tripped George and he fell. He squirmed and shouted. Shaking with laughter, he rolled down the hill. Helen ran after him. For just a moment she stopped in the darkness. There is no way of knowing what woman's thoughts went through her mind but, when the bottom of the hill was reached and she came up to the boy, she took his arm and walked beside him in dignified silence. For some reason they could not have explained they had both got from their silent evening together the thing needed. Man or boy, woman or girl, they had for a moment taken hold of the thing that makes the mature life of men and women in the modern world possible.

Departure

Young George Willard got out of bed at four in the morning. It was April and the young tree leaves were just coming out of their buds. The trees along the residence streets in Winesburg are maple and the seeds are winged. When the wind blows they whirl crazily about, filling the air and making a carpet underfoot.

George came downstairs into the hotel office carrying a brown leather bag. His trunk was packed for departure. Since two o'clock he had been awake thinking of the journey he was about to take and wondering what he would find at the end of his journey. The boy who slept in the hotel office lay on a cot by the door. His mouth was open and he snored lustily. George crept past the cot and went out into the silent deserted main street. The east was pink with the dawn and long streaks of light climbed into the sky where a few stars still shone.

Beyond the last house on Trunion Pike in Winesburg there is a great stretch of open fields. The fields are owned by farmers who live in town and drive homeward at evening along Trunion Pike in light creaking wagons. In the fields are planted berries and small fruits. In the late afternoon in the hot summers when the road and the fields are covered with dust, a smoky haze lies over the great flat basin of land. To look across it is like looking out across the sea. In the spring when the land is green the effect is somewhat different. The land becomes a wide green billiard table on which tiny human insects toil up and down.

All through his boyhood and young manhood George Willard had been in the habit of walking on Trunion Pike. He had been in the midst of the great open place on winter nights when it was covered with snow and only the moon looked down at him; he had been there in the fall when bleak winds blew and on summer evenings when the air vibrated with the song of insects. On the April morning he wanted to go there again, to walk again in the silence. He did walk to where the road dipped down by a little stream two miles from town and then turned and walked silently back again. When he got to Main Street clerks were sweeping the sidewalks before the stores. "Hey, you George. How does it feel to be going away?" they asked.

The westbound train leaves Winesburg at seven forty-five in the morning. Tom Little is conductor. His train runs from Cleveland to where it connects with a great trunk line railroad with terminals in Chicago and New York. Tom has what in railroad circles is called an "easy run." Every evening he returns to his family. In the fall and spring he spends his Sundays fishing in Lake Erie. He has a round red face and small blue eyes. He knows the people in the towns along his railroad better than a city man knows the people who live in his apartment building.

George came down the little incline from the New Willard House at seven o'clock. Tom Willard carried his bag. The son had become taller than the father.

On the station platform everyone shook the young man's hand. More than a dozen people waited about. Then they talked of their own affairs. Even Will Henderson, who was lazy and often slept until nine, had got out of bed. George was embarrassed. Gertrude Wilmot, a tall thin woman of fifty who worked in the Winesburg post office, came along the station platform. She had never before paid any attention to George. Now she stopped and put out her hand. In two words she voiced what everyone felt. "Good luck," she said sharply and then turning went on her way.

When the train came into the station George felt relieved. He scampered hurriedly aboard. Helen White came running along Main Street hoping to have a parting word with him, but he had found a seat and did not see her. When the train started Tom Little punched his ticket, grinned and, although he knew George well and knew on what adventure he was just setting out, made no comment. Tom had seen a thousand George Willards go out of their towns to the city. It was a commonplace enough incident with him. In the smoking car there was a man who had just invited Tom to go on a fishing trip to Sandusky Bay. He wanted to accept the invitation and talk over details.

George glanced up and down the car to be sure no one was looking, then took out his pocketbook and counted his money. His mind was occupied with a desire not to appear green. Almost the last words his father had said to him concerned the matter of his behavior when he got to the city. "Be a sharp one," Tom Willard had said. "Keep your eyes on your money. Be awake. That's the ticket. Don't let anyone think you're a greenhorn."

After George counted his money he looked out of the window and was surprised to see that the train was still in Winesburg.

The young man, going out of his town to meet the adventure of life, began to think but he did not think of anything very big or dramatic. Things like his mother's death, his departure from Winesburg, the uncertainty of his future life in the city, the serious and larger aspects of his life did not come into his mind.

He thought of little things—Turk Smollet wheeling boards through the main street of his town in the morning, a tall woman, beautifully gowned, who had once stayed overnight at his father's hotel, Butch Wheeler the lamp lighter of Winesburg hurrying through the streets on a summer evening and holding a torch in his hand, Helen White standing by a window in the Winesburg post office and putting a stamp on an envelope.

The young man's mind was carried away by his growing passion for dreams. One looking at him would not have thought him particularly sharp. With the recollection of little things occupying his mind he closed his eyes and leaned back in the car seat. He stayed that way for a long time and when he aroused himself and again looked out of the car window the town of Winesburg had disappeared and his life there had become but a background on which to paint the dreams of his manhood.

ACKNOWLEDGMENTS

We gratefully acknowledge all those who gave permission for written material to appear in this book. We have made every effort to trace and contact copyright holders. If an error or omission is brought to our notice we will be pleased to correct the situation in future editions of this book. For further information, please contact the publisher.

Excerpt from *The Road From Coorain* by Jill Ker Conway. Copyright ©1989 by Jill Ker Conway. Used by permission of Alfred A. Knopf, a division of Random House, Inc. ❖ "Chapter 7" from *The Liars' Club* by Mary Karr. Copyright © 1955 by Mary Karr. Used by permission of Viking Penguin, a dvision of Penguin Putnam, Inc. ❖ Excerpt from *Grendel* by John Gardner. Copyright © 1971 by John Gardner. Used by permission of Alfred A. Knopf, a division of Random House, Inc. ❖ Excerpt from *A Man Called White* by Walter White. Copyright © 1947 by Jane White Viazzi. Reprinted by permission of copyright holder, Jane White Viazzi. ❖ Excerpt from *The Good Times Are Killing Me*, published by Sasquatch Books, copyright © 1988,1998 by Lynda Barry. Reprinted by permission of the author. ❖ "Don: The True Story of A Young Person" from *Happy To Be Here* by Garrison Keillor. Copyright © 1977, 1982 by Garrison Keillor. Reprinted by permission of Scribner, a Division of Simon & Schuster. ❖ Excerpt from *Once Upon the River Love* by Andrei Makine. Copyright © 1994 by Editions du Félin. Translation © copyright 1998 by Geoffrey Strachan. Reprinted from *Once Upon the Rever Love* by Andrei Makine, published by Arcade

Publishing, New York, New York. ❖ From *Sex and Death to the Age 14* by Spalding Gray. Copyright © 1986 by Spalding Gray. Used by permission of Vintage Books, a division of Random House, Inc. ❖ Excerpt from *Growing Up* by Russell Baker. Copyright © 1982 by Russell Baker. Reprinted by permission of Don Congdon Associates, Inc. ❖ "Araby" from *Dubliners* by James Joyce. Copyright © 1916 by B.W. Heubsch. Definitive text Copyright © 1967 by the estate of James Joyce. Used by permission of Viking Penguin, a division of Penguin Putnam, Inc. ❖ From *A Tree Grows in Brooklyn* by Betty Smith. Copyright © 1943, 1947 by Betty Smith. Copyright renewed 1971 by Betty Smith (Finch). Reprinted by permission of HarperCollins Publishers, Inc. ❖ Excerpt from *Train Whistle Guitar* by Albert Murray. Copyright © 1974 by Albert Murray. Reprinted with permission of The Wylie Agency. ❖ "Sophistication", "Departure" from *Winesburg, Ohio* by Sherwood Anderson. Copyright © 1919 by B.W. Huebsch; Copyright © 1947 by Eleanor Copenhaver Anderson. Used by permission of Viking Penguin, a division of Penguin Putnam, Inc.

BIBLIOGRAPHY

Anderson, Sherwood. *Winesburg, Ohio*. New York: Viking Books, 1960.

Baker, Russell. *Growing Up*. New York: Penguin Books, 1982.

Barry, Lynda. *The Good Times Are Killing Me*. Seattle, WA: Sasquatch Books, 1998.

Conway, Jill Ker. *The Road From Coorain*. New York: Vintage Books, 1990.

Gardner, John. *Grendel*. New York: Ballantine Books, 1972.

Gray, Spalding. *Sex and Death to the Age 14*. New York: Vintage Books, 1986.

Joyce, James. *Dubliners*. New York: Penguin Books, 1967.

Karr, Mary. *The Liars' Club*. New York: Penguin Books, 1995.

Keillor, Garrison. *Happy To Be Here*. New York: Penguin Books, 1983.Makine, Andrei. *Once Upon the River Love*. New York: Penguin Books, 1998.

Murray, Albert. *Train Whistle Guitar*. New York: Vintage Books, 1998.

Smith, Betty. *A Tree Grows in Brooklyn*. New York: Perennial Books, 1998.

White, Walter. *A Man Called White*. New York: Viking Books, 1948.

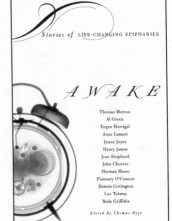